Freeing
The Light of Soul

Blair Little

Livance Inform Inc.
Publisher

Cover photo:Reality and Reflection

If you are unable to obtain this book from your local bookseller, you may order directly from the publisher:

Livance Inform Inc.
7173 Skyline Close
Saanichton,BC,Canada V8M 1M4
www.livanceinform.com
livanceinform@shaw.ca

or from:

Trafford Publishing
2404 Douglas St.
Victoria,BC,Canada V8T 4L7
Bookstore www.trafford.com

Printed in Victoria, Canada
National Library of Canada Cataloguing in Publication Data

Little, Blair, 1931-
        Freeing the light of soul / Blair Little.
ISBN 1-4120-0453-5
        I. Title.
PS8573.I832F74 2003   C813'.6   C2003-903105-5
PR9199.4.L574F74 2003

Trafford Catalogue #03-0822   www.trafford.com/robots/03-0822.html

| 10 | 9 | 8 | 7 | 6 | 5 | 4 | 3 |

Freeing
The Light Of Soul

The word went out:
The time is now; the Prince is on his throne,
His Kingdom is reclaimed.
The people rejoiced.

Their peace had set them free.

Preface

In every presentation of spiritual concepts, there are elements of speculation and uncertainty. This story is no exception. That is why readers should feel free to challenge what is proposed here about the esoteric world. The story is meant to provoke readers to consider new possibilities and think more deeply in shaping their own view of reality. Perhaps it will elicit an intuitive registration of a new knowing, or a fresh opening to a greater scope of the mind. That would be its greatest contribution.

Many people have helped in the telling of this story. There are those who read earlier drafts and offered many valuable suggestions about both content and style: Daniel Krummenacher, Danielle Vecchio, Gloria Kelly, Patricia Benesh, Jan Mattsson, Helen Collicutt and Dorothea Vickery. There are also the many teachers I have had the good fortune to meet along the Path who have helped me learn the way. Then there are those who have tested many of the story's ideas in workshops and retreats and helped to make them more understandable. To all, my deepest gratitude, and my declaration that I assume full responsibility for any deficiencies in the end result.

Finally, I am especially grateful to Peggy Little, my partner in life, for her editorial help and her constant encouragement.

Blair Little

Two Heritages

Soul Heritage: *Aiya*	Socio-physical Heritage: *The Cameron Family*

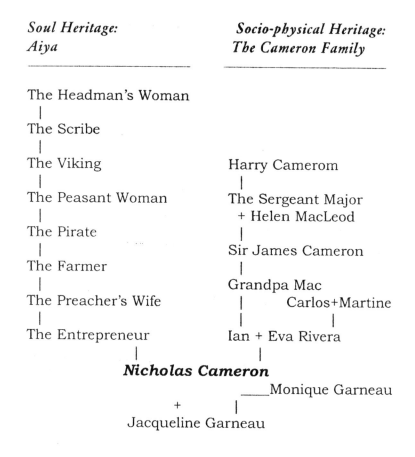

The Headman's Woman
|
The Scribe
|
The Viking   Harry Camerom
| |
The Peasant Woman   The Sergeant Major
| + Helen MacLeod
The Pirate |
| Sir James Cameron
The Farmer |
| Grandpa Mac
The Preacher's Wife | Carlos+Martine
| | |
The Entrepreneur   Ian + Eva Rivera
            | |
    Nicholas Cameron
                              ____Monique Garneau
            + |
    Jacqueline Garneau

Chapter One

The Long Way Home

"Do you have any last words of advice, my Senior, before I make the descent?"

"You do know what this next incarnation is about, Aiya, my friend of old?"

"Yes, my Senior, I do." In the subjective realm, the two souls, being energy centers, communicated mind to mind without the hindrance of a physical brain. Although their thought waves were on the abstract plane, far above the tone of personalty's thoughts, they could convey meaning with clarity. It was a high order telepathy.

"The human form with which you are aligning – it meets well your requirements?

"Yes, my Senior. The body should be healthy and it is a fine family."

"And astrologically?"

"We are well positioned. The overall resonance is strong, my Senior. We are quite a good match as far as I can see, although it is still early to tell for sure."

"Let's hope it is right for you, then, Aiya my old friend. You know if it goes well you will complete the requirements to advance to the next rank of the soul world.

"Yes sir. I understand. With this experience, my handling of the human form could progress enough that my Center of Knowing can take its rightful place as the primary energy of the personality."

"It will demand your full concentration, Aiya, and every ounce of will your core can muster."

"Yes, my Senior."

"You will be bold, my friend, won't you?"

"Yes, my Senior, I will be bold."

"Take care, then, my colleague, and go with my love."

Aiya withdrew from the presence of the Senior and concentrated on the logistics of the transition that lay ahead. If he got it right, this incarnation could be a decisive battle on the long road through the cycles of many incarnations. It was crucial for the plan to be followed with care. The prospect was both daunting and invigorating.

A thought wave from another soul intervened. "We are going together, Aiya."

"Together indeed, Ohruu. On the same wave of purpose."

"It is unlikely our physical bodies will meet. I see you are lining up with an English family."

"And you are on your way to France."

"Whether or not our physical lives are close, Aiya, we will continue in close energy contact. Since we are part of the same soul group we have a wide band of common vibrational resonance. That makes for a strong magnetic attraction between us."

"Perhaps, then, our vehicles will find one another."

"Perhaps. Perhaps not. Either way, our magnetic link means we combine our strength of will. When our fields merge, we are each more than twice as strong as we are as individuals."

"We'll need that extra strength this time. I mean, really need it."

"That's true. It will be a stretch for both of us, Aiya. A long stretch."

"You know what it means if we succeed, Ohruu?"

"Yes, my colleague, I know. It means we will be free."

"Can you imagine, Ohruu? Free. Never again to take second place to the will of personality. Could it be true?"

"It is still a maybe, Aiya, but I think we can do it. I think we are well on our way home."

"Home." The thought illuminated Aiya's field with the light of the oversoul, the soul of humanity. "When I think of home, Ohruu, everything is different. The magnetic attraction of the oversoul penetrates to my very core. It wills me to keep on seeking."

Both felt the almost painful longing for healing, for wholeness, for the freedom from the weight of persona impurities. It was the driving impulse behind the soul's cycle of incarnation after incarnation. And it was the deep source of all the longings and desires of a human personality.

"It has taken so many incarnations to find our way back, Ohruu. How many times have we endured the descent, do you think? A few hundred?"

"More."

"They're like a long dream that I can't quite remember. There are only a handful of marker incidents along the way."

"We lose track of the details, Aiya, because our journey has been just like that - a continuous stream of experiences - learning, absorbing, and learning again."

"Learning. Are we so slow to learn? How many lessons does it take?"

"It depends on how well we learn the assigned lesson of each descent."

"I know some lessons take several incarnations."

"And some we catch on the first try."

"We were very slow to learn, Ohruu, in those, oh so many early tries."

"The substance of the human bodies we had to work with was very dense in our early incarnations, Aiya, and we were new at the learning game. We moved faster in the later trials as we got better at bringing our light through the constriction of the lower vibrations of a physical body and the attendant energy fields."

"Also, the planet's pace of evolution has speeded up. The energy is much stronger now."

"Yes, in the last two thousand years we have been driven by more potent impressions."

"We have had some tough lessons, Ohruu, you and I, learning to bring spirit into matter."

"And that is why we are here. Our role is to infuse our refined qualities into the matter of the human physical plane. We've been at it since the first spark of soul inhabited animal man."

"Our work with humanity is still a long way from being finished. It is not easy to adjust the dense substance of human forms, enough even to register our presence, let alone bring our presence into full expression."

"Do you remember, Aiya, the first time your impulse registered as a direct response in your human vehicle?"

"Yes I do. It was many thousands of years ago - one of those notable incidents in the long dream."

Chapter Two

The Headman's Woman

The fur-clad figures made their way across the ridges
and plains of the arctic sea ice, each following in the
footsteps of the one in front, the band's Headman
leading the way. The men had been gone for four
days looking for food for the starving band. The
women and children stood and watched them
approach, straining their eyes in the mid-day twilight
to see if the hunters were bringing any carcasses
back to the camp. They saw none. In stoic silence,
they turned and moved as one body toward their ice
shelters. They separated into family groups and
crawled inside where they huddled together under
their furs.

As the Headman reached the shelters, he
growled a string of curses and called to his woman.
She emerged from the shelter and went scrambling
obediently to get the band's last scrap of food which
the women had carefully saved for the hunters. She
brought it to the lee side of a shelter where the
hunters had slumped together. They tore at the few
pieces of raw seal meat like ravenous dogs. She
watched them for a few minutes, trying to sort out
the vague thoughts that started to form in her mind,
then gave up thinking and trudged back to her
family shelter.

Something had happened to the animals along
their coast - they knew not what. Finding food was
harder than it had ever been. Over the past three
years, they had pushed far beyond their traditional

hunting areas and still they had not found the great herds of seals that had always been their livelihood. This year the animals had almost completely disappeared. The band's shaman had seen images of better hunting another two days' travel to the east, but they were afraid other bands would attack them if they went further in that direction. It had happened once to their ancestors.

The Headman's Woman, Aiya's external appearance, gazed around the shelter at the smallest children snuggled in their mother's furs, too weak to hold up their heads, almost too weak to breath. Her maternal instinct kicked up. "This is wrong," she mumbled to herself. "We can't just sit here waiting to die. Someone has to do something or our band will no longer exist." The woman's thought, based on instinct, stirred her mind to reflect her soul's vibration of will. Her corresponding will to live penetrated her emotional body and activated a surge of anger that erupted in her gut. The woman sat up straight, unusually alert. Her mind formulated a basic thought that became an urge to action. Her body rocked forward. "Get food," she mumbled to herself. "Get food."

Until now, she had been living instinctively within the aura of the band, an undifferentiated element. The band had been her identity, her meaning, her very physical being. She and the band were one and the same thing. But now, suddenly, she found herself looking *at* the band, not *being* the band. She became vaguely aware of her individuality and had a strange and uncomfortable sense of personal responsibility. She had to do something.

She grunted and pushed herself to her knees. She hesitated for a moment, perplexed by this urge to act, but quickly put her confusion aside. She crawled out of her ice shelter and stalked over to the men as they ate. She grabbed the Headman by the shoulders and shook him as hard as she could, haranguing him to do something to save them. He was the Head. It was his responsibility, she yelled.

She had never behaved this way before and she startled the Headman. He swung his arm abruptly to shake her off, glared at her for a moment, then turned back to chew on his last mouthful of meat.

She knew it was hopeless. He would just wait until life presented itself to them, in its own time, in its own way. If they all died, then that was what was to happen. "Ocean in charge." the Head declared, speaking in grunting monosyllables and gestures. "Ocean. He decides."

His declaration was not good enough for the woman. She slammed her fists on his shoulders, croaked a disgusted "Agh," and turned her back on him. She stamped determinedly back to the shelter, packed her sleeping furs over her shoulder, picked up a spear and, with a few words to the huddled women and children, crawled out of the shelter and trudged away toward the east.

"Where you go, woman?"

She glanced back at him but didn't answer. The Head growled louder. "Not go east, stupid woman. That direction go nowhere. Enemies kill."

She walked straight on, not hesitating. "Come back." he signed. She ignored him. "I order." he roared. No response. He threw a dismissing hand in her direction and gave a throaty curse, then turned back to the men, his shrug saying, "She go. She die." He finished the matter with a concluding, "She gone."

After three days, the woman reappeared, dragging the carcasses of three seals behind her. The first to see her shouted into the ice shelters to alert the others who lay together, weak and dispirited, ready for death. The Headman stopped her before she got to the others and grabbed the meat away from her with a scowl. She had undermined his position in the band and now he would have to rebuild his credibility. He supervised the cutting and dividing of the food while the woman hunter sat alone to one side, eating what had been given to her.

The next day the Headman announced the band would move east where he had determined, after consultation with the shaman, there would be better hunting and no enemies. The woman remained silent and followed at the back of the band. She was no longer the Headman's Woman. Even though she had saved their lives, the Headman's manner and gestures directed the band to ostracize her because she had become different from them, somehow no longer physically of the band. Her behavior could not be comprehended.

A few years later, the woman registered another reflection of Aiya's will vibration and her mind formulated another initiative for the band. She had the idea they should seek even better hunting by traveling further to the unknown east. Under the guise of following the Headman's leadership, the band went with her to a totally new land six weeks' travel to the east where they found animals in plentiful supply. There in that distant land, at the very old age of fifty-one, she became ill and unable to follow the nomadic life of the band. When the band gathered up their belongings to move on to their next hunting ground, she remained seated by herself on an ice shelf. A few came over to touch her on the arm before leaving. Within hours of their departure, she died a normal death where the band had abandoned her.

The actions of the Headman's Woman had shown the first tiny glimmer of the light of soul penetrating the density of the human form. For the first time, the human vehicle Aiya inhabited had become conscious of herself as an individual, recognizing in herself an identity which was distinct from the band, able to create distinctive thoughts. Primitive though her consciousness was, her mental initiative represented

8

a milestone in the soul's grasp of the personality. For Aiya, it was the first time a personality showed awareness of a unique self. It was a notable event in the long road from soul's first appearance in the human form.

In the context of the long road ahead, however, the success with the Headman's Woman was a very small step. It would take many more incarnations for Aiya to bring a human form to full self-consciousness. To then take the form onward to full mental funtioning at the highest level would require still another series of difficult incarnating ventures.

Chapter Three

The Scribe

The Roman soldier swung his sword from side to side in wide sweeps, threatening to slice the flesh of any spectator who came too close. The soldier and his fellow legionnaires were clearing the road as the Emperor's procession, a long caravan of horses and carriages carrying courtiers and porters, entered the town. "Get back! Get back! The Emperor is coming!" he shouted. "Pay your respects or pay with your head, you miserable dogs."

Among the courtiers riding in a carriage just behind the Emperor's was Aiya's human form - an introverted, servile scribe. The scribe was an obsequious note-taker who was recording the story of his sovereign's journey into Gaul.

It had taken Aiya more than a hundred incarnations to advance its command of personality beyond animating a primitive notion of self, as expressed by the Headman's Woman, to achieving the focused self-concern of this deeply fearful but literate fourth century appearance. In this incarnation, the personality might be sufficiently aligned that it could register enough of Aiya's vibration to break through the scribe's fear-charged astral barrier and release the mental equipment for even a small measure of clear, objective thought. Aiya's ever present vibration was like a patient probe seeking to exploit any opening the personality allowed, seeking to promote soul's presence.

"Give way, there. Stand back." The soldiers forced a wide swath through the crowds. Whenever the procession paused for rest or food, the scribe pulled out his wax covered tablets and metal pen and wrote how pleased the people were to see their ruler, this powerful near-god who governed half the world as they knew it. He wrote about how popular the Emperor was among his soldiers, and how welcome he was among the local administrators of the empire. The writing was crafted with care for the eyes of the suspicious audience of ruling patricians in Rome, so the random assaults on the locals, the complaints of the administrators, and the grumbling of the soldiers went unreported. They did not need to know those details back home. Nor did they need to know how much the Emperor feared the foreigners.

From the legions at the back of the column, a frantic call for help echoed up the line to the troops in the lead. "An army of outlaws is attacking. Send back reinforcements." Mounted soldiers wheeled and charged to the rear, scattering onlookers as they sped to the attack. The Emperor's own guards closed more tightly around his carriage, nervously eyeing the crowds up and down the road. The timid scribe, seized with terror, sank back into the corner of the carriage in which he rode with two other attendants. He secured his codex and pen in his satchel and hugged his arms across his body.

"We should not have come here," the scribe murmured to his two companions.

"You are not afraid are you, you worm?" a fat courtier chided him.

"Be silent," the scribe whispered.

"Be silent? Is that the best you can do, scribe?" The fat one turned to the courtier beside him and snickered, "This worm is afraid of his own shadow." The scribe dropped his chin into his chest and scrunched lower in his seat.

On a rooftop above the procession, three men hoisted a huge block of stone and heaved it into the roadway. It landed squarely on the back part of the Emperor's carriage, narrowly missing the Emperor but buckling his carriage so the rear wheels fell off. The Emperor cringed in his carriage, frozen in fear. His guards ran about in confusion, swinging their swords and screaming at the townspeople. The scribe hugged himself even more tightly while his coach companions beseeched their gods to save them.

The scribe's terror invoked another filament of Aiya's will. The mass of static energy, which the terror had created in the scribe's solar plexus, attracted an increase in the voltage of the soul's vibration. The filament of soul will pierced the mass of static to the center, loosening the static's hold on the scribe's energy system, dissipating the portion of static highlighted by the attack, and dissolving the paralyzing fear. The scribe felt his whole body shake and straighten as though hit by lightening. Soul's will had broken through a layer of the astral barrier and registered a higher level of presence in the personality's expression.

The scribe, unaware of his underlying energy revision, involuntarily straightened up on his seat, shaking and momentarily weak. He was confused and afraid of what was happening to him. Within a minute, though, the confusion subsided and he became alert and confident. His now stronger mind was able to override his fears and become an instrument of his selfishness. He rapidly assessed how he could gain something for himself from the chaotic situation. It clicked. He leapt out of his carriage, ran forward to the traumatized Emperor, grabbed him by the belt and pulled him back to his own carriage.

"Follow this carriage!" he yelled to the stunned guards. They immediately obeyed him. The scribe helped the Emperor into the carriage and barked orders to the driver. "Down that side road to the left." The driver whipped the horses to a gallop and followed the scribe's instruction. "Do not stop until we have traveled two leagues," the scribe yelled.

"What has taken him?" the fat courtier whispered. His companion blinked and shook his head.

When the driver eventually pulled the carriage to a halt, the scribe pointed to the two courtiers in the carriage and commanded them, "Remove yourselves from the Emperor's presence. Go find yourself a horse." When they objected, he mimicked, "You are not afraid are you, you worms?"

"Of course not," they blustered.

"Ironheads.' the scribe snarled. "Out! Your words do not obscure your rumbling guts."

"Head north." he commanded the driver and the guards. "Keep a sharp lookout." He settled back on the seat opposite the Emperor, lowering his eyes, waiting for his sovereign's gratitude. He looked up briefly and the Emperor gave him a slight nod of the head. The scribe was beside himself with pleasure, basking in warm thoughts of the rewards which might flow from the Emperor for his life-saving action. A servant of his own would be fine, he thought, or perhaps larger quarters. At the end of the day, settled for the night in safe territory, the scribe pulled out his codex and continued writing dutifully about the triumphal reception given the Emperor by the Gauls.

On their return to Rome, the Emperor gave the scribe an administrative post, a reward even greater than the scribe had dared hope for - it put him into a much higher stratum of society. In the years that followed, the former scribe's personality continued to interpret Aiya's impulse as selfish ambition. The astral breakthrough allowed the man to think more clearly and to find more clever ways to satisfy his selfishness. He learned to become a rather accomplished head of his department, and more importantly, he learned to survive in the midst of the scheming, ambitious crowd at court. No longer the timid acolyte, Aiya's form now focused brashly on self promotion while at the same time appearing to be acting solely on behalf of the Emperor. The personality was strengthening and the mind was beginning to take hold.

It was another distinctive, core-etching incarnation for Aiya – a memory in the stream of the dream.

Chapter Four

The Viking

"Icebergs!" the lookout shouted. "Icebergs! Heave to or we're doomed." His alarm spread through the ship. "We're going to collide." He waved frantically to the Viking chieftain in the stern. "Take down the sail," the lookout cried. The crew sprang to the sail lines.

"Stand fast! The sail stays," the chieftain shouted. "You!" He shook his fist at the lookout. "You oyster-hearted weakling! You get back up in the prow and keep a keen eye for land, or I'll break your neck." The chieftain allowed no weakness in his crew. "The rest of you, get back on the oars. I know how to deal with icebergs."

The knorr strained up and over the mountains of the North Atlantic Ocean, its square sail full, its pliant planks and timbers working with the twisting forces of the sea. She was heavily loaded with a cargo of cattle feed, meal, iron, and other trade goods which were in high demand in the Greenland settlements the Vikings had established years before. She carried a crew of twenty-four as well as a few would-be settlers.

The chieftain, who was Aiya's vehicle for this incarnation, stood tall, one arm wrapped around the steer-board. He stared defiantly into the storm as though he could beat it back with the strength of his will. He was determined to hold to the most direct course in order to be the first of the spring traders to arrive and have the choice of the ivory tusks of the walrus and narwhale which were so highly prized back in Europe.

The strength of the chieftain's personality was the product of Aiya's five human experiences since the breakthrough that came with the transformation of the scribe. Now the form was strong enough for another step in the long process of refinement.

The bow heaved up on a huge wave and the ship shuddered and shifted sideways before plunging smoothly through. "Man overboard!" a crewman screamed. The chieftain made no move as he considered whether he should bother to do anything about it. He quickly weighed the benefits of staying the course or turning to save the man. He decided.

"Take the helm and bring the ship around," the chieftain shouted to his brother who was standing next to him. To a cousin he commanded, "Get the afterboat into the water." The weighing of benefits didn't count - it was simply the right thing for a chieftain to do. With that thought, his mind registered a strong vibration of will and he became totally focused on saving the man.

He threw off his heavy cloak and dove into the cold black ocean. He fought through white-capped waves and swam with powerful strokes toward the head he could now and then see bobbing on the surface. He grabbed his crewman by the hair and kept him floating on his back until the men in the afterboat picked them up.

The decision to rescue the crewman arose from a stimulation from Aiya's vibration of the chieftain's unconscious notion of a leader's duty to his followers – a first glimmer of personal responsibility for the welfare of others, a faint reflection of the energy of love. After the fact, however, the chieftain consciously marked it up as an increase in the debt he was owed by his crew.

Over the years, Aiya's vibration continued to press steadily on a now more receptive personality, urging it into responsible thought and action. These were still early stages of soul's influence, however, and in the eyes of the chieftain, his good works had to be repaid through a show of respect and a vow of allegiance from those he helped. When the chieftain was forty-seven years old, a repayment he expected was not forthcoming. In the ensuing inter-family feud, he was killed and his family was banished from the community - a karmic lesson, Aiya noted, to be carried forward to a future life.

It was necessary, Aiya knew, for the personality to become a strong and integrated vehicle which could stand the refined vibration of soul's invasion. In the early phases of development, however, as the scribe and chieftain showed, the first threads of personality strength gave a poor translation of soul's qualities and made the vehicle extremely self-centered. Nevertheless, this was progress. In subsequent phases of the strengthening, as the emotional and mental bodies became somewhat quieter and more orderly under the weathering of challenging incarnations, personality would start to show a better reflection of soul's qualities and the self-centeredness would subside.

But that was for the future.

Chapter Five

The Peasant Woman

The Mongol warrior smiled with satisfaction, having found what he was looking for. He dismounted and approached the peasant cottage beside the field of wheat. Some forty paces away from the cottage he tied his horse to an apple tree and watched a young peasant woman washing clothes in a large tub by the back door. This would make a fine wife, he thought to himself – a sturdy body, a round face, a good worker. *Yes, she is the one I will have*, he decided. *She will come with me.*

The woman, Aiya's thirteenth century human form, sensed the intruder's presence and looked up. When she saw the marauder, she let out a startled cry and scuttled quickly into the cottage out of sight. She closed and bolted the door, shaking with fright. These invaders had stormed out of the east and into the grain fields of the steppes, destroying everything in their path without a speck of compassion. They burned cities, killed thousands and took whatever they wanted. They had already killed her father and mother and three brothers. She despised them, saw them as vicious and cruel animals. Nothing could stop them – their horsemanship and fighting skills were more than ordinary armies could withstand. And their numbers - they came in hordes. And here was one in her yard. Coming to kill her.

The warrior left his horse and, still smiling, walked slowly, casually, toward the cottage, stroking his horsewhip with stubby fingers. At the cottage door he hardly broke stride as he lifted a thick short leg and jammed it right through the boards of the door. The woman screamed and the Mongol felt a severe, sharp pain across his ankle. He cried out in anguish and quickly withdrew his leg, hopping on one foot. He was smiling no more.

Inside, the woman wielded an iron poker she had taken from the cooking fire and was ready to defend herself. She screamed at the horrid invader, "Get out. Get out of my yard. I'll kill you!" The door was jolted again from the outside and the hinges loosened. "I warn you. Get away from here or I'll kill you." He didn't understand her language but understood her message. There was another blow to the door. And another. The door was splintering. The woman prayed fervently as her Eastern Orthodoxy had taught her and that prayerful invocation opened her emotional center to Aiya's vibration. The will aspect of the vibration stiffened the woman's backbone. With renewed fury, she screamed again at the menace. Another thump from outside. She waived the poker over her head and waited for a piece of human flesh to appear again so she could smash it. The sturdy body which the horseman had admired was accompanied by a sturdy will which gained strength as her every prayer summoned another high frequency filament of will.

The invader continued with deliberation and persistence to batter the door until the hinges finally gave way. Now he could see the woman waving the poker at him, daring him to come closer. He glared at her and boldly stepped forward, ready to duck if necessary. It wasn't necessary. She stepped back. He stepped forward again and she dropped the poker. She could not hit him. In the distance, he was an enemy, a murderer. Up close, he was a human being. She could smash a booted leg. She could not smash a face. The infusion of Aiya's energy of will had also

19

FREEING THE LIGHT OF SOUL

installed a first glimpse of compassion – an important and memorable achievement.

The woman ran to the far corner of the cottage and cowered against the wall. "No. Please. No," she cried. The broad-shouldered attacker glared at her forbiddingly as he limped slowly toward her, his ankle swollen and aching. When he was close, she whimpered and cried and pressed back against the wall. "Please. Please. Don't kill me. Please." He grabbed her wrist, turned, and dragged her to the door. She struggled, kicking him, hitting him with her free hand, trying to wriggle out of his grasp, sagging to the floor to slow his progress, all to no avail. His grip was a tight clamp she could not break. He just kept walking, out the door, across the yard, dragging her as though she were a sack of potatoes. In one motion he threw her across the withers of his horse and swung himself up to ride.

That was the violent start of their twenty years together in a relationship which evolved while they rode with the horde as it swarmed across the steppes and into Eastern Europe. For three years she constantly fought him and regularly tried to escape. She finally gave that up and for the next several years was a sullen, unwilling inhabitant of his camp. Eventually though, for her own emotional survival, she relented and began to join with the flow of camp life. Her change of perspective made way for a partial resonance in her heart center of the energy of Aiya's love aspect. With the prodding of that energy impulse, she gradually found an inner strength which allowed her to see the faint light of the human being within her warrior kidnapper. A tolerable truce settled around them. Their lives fell into place: they were husband and wife - he was master, she was servant. The couple died in an epidemic within a few weeks of one another.

Although the events of life can be tumultuous in the consciousness of the personality, they are but the warp and woof of the fabric soul weaves as it learns to master the human form. Aiya knew the most traumatic lives for the personality usually led to the greatest advance in the soul's learning. The peasant woman's life was a case in point. What looked on the outside like conflict, was on the inside a tempering of the steel of personality will, a dim reflection of soul's will aspect. What looked on the outside like resignation and submission, was on the inside an introduction of a hint of compassion, a reflection of soul's love aspect.

Over the years, the woman had been able to find the beginnings of inner peace in the face of an outer life of violence. It was the first time one of Aiya's vehicles had learned, even though not consciously, to arrive at an inner solution to external provocations. It was evidence of another step forward on the road to full self-consciousness.

Chapter Six

The Pirate

There was hardly a sound as the ship rode at anchor while the crew slept below in their bunks. Only the full moon was witness to the man approaching in a small dinghy.

He slipped under the stern, past the anchor chain, and came along the starboard side beneath the rail. Silently he pulled himself up onto the deck and tied the dinghy to a cleat. Then he crept forward through the stacks of cargo to the fore deck where he spotted a sailor lying on his back, apparently staring at the moon. The sailor jerked up when he saw the intruder, but before he could cry out a massive fist smashed into his skull. A lookout sitting a few yards away in the bow turned with curiosity toward the muffled sound. He received one blow to the head and joined his companion on the deck.

The intruder quickly dragged the two bodies to the rail and heaved them overboard. He waited a moment to see if the splashes would draw attention. Nothing.

Now he went to the stern and gave a long low whistle. Three more dinghies materialized out of the darkness, each carrying four men. In a moment all were aboard. Half of them started preparing the ship to sail while the other half stood by the hatches grabbing the crew as they scurried up on deck. In efficient style they cracked them on the head one by one and threw them overboard to drown.

"Get the gold into my dinghy, you lot," ordered the leader. "The rest you can divide any way you want. Then sail this ship and its cargo off to any buyer you can find. Get it done and be back within a month." The leader of the pirates was fifty years of age, a barrel-chested, wild-eyed strongman. Among his band were his three sons, all in their twenties and just as strong as their father.

The oldest son was Aiya's form, an incarnation during which the personality would develop the capacity to go beyond self-absorption and see the self with more mental objectivity – to be a better observer of the self. It would be no easy task, Aiya knew, given the young man's start in life and his overwhelming self-centeredness.

"Look at our fortune," the heir apparent said to his younger brothers as they counted their take from their latest prize. "Our father is a great man."

"Our father is fearless, brothers. Can we match him?"

"For all his greatness, I will be greater," the older brother declared.

"So you think, brother. We will see."

"Is it not marvelous, my brothers?" the youngest enthused. "Everyone on this coast respects our father."

"They are afraid of him, and they will be afraid of me," the oldest proclaimed. "He is like a king. He rules this coast, and so will I. And lands beyond."

"You spout, brother," mocked the second, "but you have yet to show the greatness of our father."

"That is all our father cares about, you know," the youngest observed. "All he cares about is that people see him as the great man he is. He expects us to become just like him."

"Mark my words, you two. I will be just like him – and more!" boasted the oldest brother. He looked up at the sky and thrust his chin forward. "I have the strength of ten men and the courage of ten lions," he shouted to the universe. "God will give me the supremacy of this coast in greater measure than my father's." He drove his fist into the air. "I shall be a greater man than he." Aiya could see this man, his vehicle, was either going to die young or his ego was going to crash from a great height to discover the meaning of his inner life. Aiya's pre-incarnation plan aimed for the latter outcome.

Personal aggrandizement was a common goal among heads of families of fourteenth century Genoa. In this family, however, there was an extraordinary dose of violence that accompanied the fire of exaggerated Latin machismo. The patriarch had killed at least forty men, perhaps many more than that – he didn't keep track of his killings, they were so incidental to his quest for gold and a heroic identity.

At the height of his success, the father died suddenly of a heart attack and his eldest son, at thirty years of age, succeeded him as head of the pirate gang. For twenty years the son lived determinedly the life his father had taught him. He earned a reputation that was fully the equal of his father's. Then something happened which devastated him. His own twenty-year-old son was killed on a raid against the merchants of a coastal town.

His anger was explosive and he spewed blame in all directions. He blamed one of the merchants for his son's death and so went back and set fire to the town. He blamed his gang members for bungling the raid and physically beat several of them. He blamed his dead father for creating the family culture of violence and smashed the sketch of the man that hung on the wall. In his anger and frustration, he cursed his dead grandfather for siring his father, he cursed the church and its God for not protecting his son, he cursed his poor wife for not making the son more alert, he cursed life and the unfair way it unfolded.

The pirate's crisis of meaning was an opportunity for Aiya's ever waiting impulse to restructure the pirate's thought pattern. In the midst of one particularly violent outburst directed at his wife, the absurdity of his attack reached such a height, it crashed under its own weight. Aiya's vibration surged through the man's heart like an electric shock. It blasted his mind into clarity. His anger evaporated like a cloud of steam. Then tears welled up in his eyes. He slumped onto a chair and slammed his fist on the kitchen table. "It is all wrong," he groaned. "All wrong, wrong, wrong." He looked up at his wife. "I am the one," he wailed. "I am the one."

"What are you saying, my husband?"

"I am the one. I am the one to blame. No one else." His mind looked deep into his emotional turmoil, cutting through like a surgeon's knife. "It is my fault." He sobbed like a child. "Our son's death. My fault. My responsibility." He banged his forehead on the table. Looking up through his tears he moaned, "Look at me, my wife. Look at my pitiful life. Look at how I have sinned. I am a mountain of sin." He threw his head back with his arms outstretched as though on a cross. He closed his eyes and lamented, "Oh God, I am unworthy of your care. I don't deserve to live. I beseech you, Oh Lord, cleanse the earth of my presence." He collapsed across the table in agony.

When the priest visited the household the following week, the pirate's wife told him, "The shock of it has walled him off from everybody. It is as though he died."

"Does he speak to no one?"

"No one. Not even to me. He just sits in the garden and stares at the trees."

"Have patience, my lady. God works in strange ways sometimes."

As was its way, Aiya took little note of the life circumstances of its outer form when the form's evolutionary maturity was at the level of the pirate's. The soul attended only to being a responsive energy vibration when the personality, of its own accord, reached upward to a higher frequency. It was the role of the pirate's personality to find the strength to pull itself out of its depression. If it succeeded, it would be a stronger, more competent vehicle for Aiya's further, higher frequency influence. If it didn't, the soul would wait for another chance, perhaps in a later incarnation.

"Will he ever be the same again, my priest?" the woman asked.

"Let us hope not, dear lady. Let us hope not."

After two months of silence, her husband came in from the garden one morning and stood at the door of the kitchen. His wife looked up from her baking. He said nothing.

"What is it?" she asked, waiting. His eyes were different – they were still, contented. "Say something." She was a little frightened. "Are you paralyzed? Can you not speak?"

"It is time to stop the cycle," he said calmly. "I am leaving this life."

"No!" She recoiled from his announcement. "You can't do that."

"Please now, do as I say. Take our three daughters and go to your father's home. You will be free of my sinful life. I will give you enough gold for all of you to live comfortably for the rest of your lives. The rest of my fortune, I will give to the church."

"And you?"

"I am leaving this life for another."

The pirate joined a monastery, and within the cloistered grounds he lived in celibacy, in silence and in poverty. In the stillness of the monastic life, the repentant monk prayed silently for hours and hours every day, chanting silently and continuously,

26

"Forgive me, Oh Lord, for I knew not what I did. I prostrate myself before you in all humility and in complete obedience."

The pirate's repentance and surrender had the effect of an invitation to soul. The prayers relaxed some of the barriers to Aiya's presence and the soul's influence pressed steadily into the pirate's consciousness for the remaining twenty-five years of his life. Aiya counted it as another special voyage in form.

Chapter Seven

The Farmer

It was a runaway. Manes flying, ears back, eyes wild, the team of horses raced down the winding road, still attached to an elegant coach which bounced its passengers off their seats and threw them from side to side. The driver fought unsuccessfully for control and was getting ready to jump to save himself. Disaster seemed imminent until a farmer, Aiya's form, dashed out of a field where he had been plowing and stood in the middle of the road to challenge the oncoming charge. He raised his arms and waived at them vigorously. He jumped up and down and shouted at the team as it bore down on him. Confused, the horses shoved against each other and slowed enough for the farmer to grab the traces on one of the horses. The team dragged him along the rough road until his yanking at the bit of one of the horses finally brought the runaway to a halt.

The farmer had acted impulsively, without thought for himself, to save the passengers from harm. He was lucky he hadn't been killed. The passengers, it turned out, were of the nobility and, to no one's surprise, they took his heroic actions as their due. Without a thank-you to the farmer, they pulled themselves together and instructed their driver to proceed.

The farmer may not have been a nobleman but he could have noble thoughts about life, and being a farmer gave him lots of time to think as he worked

28

his fields. Some days he would leave his valley and climb the mountains high above his village, above the alpine meadows where his neighbors grazed their cows in the summer, above the tree line to the bare ridges and sheer rock faces which rose cleanly into the sky. Here he would find a comfortable ledge in the warm sun and sit for hours, setting free his noble thoughts in the royal halls of his majestic mountains. Here, within the aura of Aiya's encouraging impulse, his mind would evolve and mature, new questions would be born and new answers would appear.

On the day of the runaway, he sat on the sunny ledge and wondered what force had propelled him into personal danger. In the fine energy of the mountains, it was easier for Aiya's finer frequency to animate the farmer's mental field. With that finer vibration, the farmer's thoughts reached out to a wider scope of the universal intelligence. His mind wandered into philosophical abstractions and back again to earth. *I wasn't saving a member of my family. You would risk your life for them, of course, because they were your flesh and blood. And you would try to save your friends – close friends, at least, for they were nearly your flesh and blood. But those people in the coach were strangers, foreigners in fact - they came from the next valley.*

So, why did I do it? I am just a simple hardworking farmer. I hold no position of responsibility for the welfare of those passengers - I am neither their master nor their serf. And I sought no favor of them, no reward, not even a hero's approbation. I could see others might act from those motives. But those were not my motives. Why did I do it?

The farmer's searching questions and his quiet contemplation invited another filament of Aiya's vibration. Resonating with soul's impulse expanded the farmer's heart center, giving a further refinement

29

to the mental field and extending the range of its sensitivity. The farmer began to absorb from the intelligence of the universe a subtle yet real awareness of the attractive force of the universal love impulse. His thoughts flowed. *I wonder - is there something within a human being that connects him to other human beings – to all human beings? Are there some hidden strings that pull at us, that touch our hearts? Is there some hidden influence that prompted me to act the way I did, to act as though they were my flesh and blood?*

Another filament of Aiya's love impulse took hold of the form. It brought the fact of humanity's connecting network to the farmer's attention – a first realization beyond self-consciousness to a glimpse of soul awareness.

After stopping the runaway, the farmer went more often into his mountains to ponder the meaning of his life, sometimes even to the neglect of his fields. In that rare atmosphere and that infinite silence, the farmer's mental field continued to refine in resonance to Aiya's influence. His mystical senses deepened. His soul awareness strengthened. He had neither the words nor any authority's explanation for his new perspective, but he knew his life had changed.

Chapter Eight

The Preacher's Wife

"Hurry, Nathaniel! Hold on tight to my hand. We must hurry home." The young mother pulled her small son behind her, forcing her way along the shoreline against the blast of the Atlantic storm. The roar of the wind and waves magnified her fear. "God, help us," she cried as she fought to get back to their little East Coast settlement.

The woman was Aiya's instrument and her call for God's intervention invoked the soul's vibration of will. Her personality resonated to the impulse of that vertical strand of energy, giving added fiber to her will to live. She reached deep for all of her physical strength and pressed into the raging force that tore at them. Suddenly, the howling wind picked up a giant wave and sent it crashing across their path, sweeping the two of them off their feet. As the torrent retreated, she was caught up in a pile of debris and the boy's little hand slipped from hers.

"Nathaniel! No! Dear God, No. Not Nathaniel. Oh, please God." The mother could only watch the roiling waves in horror. Her son, her only child, was gone. Swept into the ocean. "Take me, God. Not Nathaniel. Take me instead." she pleaded. She screamed in anguish at the roiling storm. "It's the devil," she croaked. "He has taken my son." Then shouting, "You evil, monstrous, marauder of the darkness. Begone, you hear! Begone!"

31

If only she had known how powerful a storm could be. The horrendous hurricane had boiled up the coast that morning thrusting the high tide before it. Blowing stronger by the hour, it piled up the ocean and sent it flooding over the land, tearing apart the rough buildings of the new settlement. Her husband had led the English settlers to this land in the New World only two years ago – there were thirty-five of them in a closely-knit religious community – and nothing like this had happened to them before. Everything was destroyed – their homes, their crops. Everything. Washed away by the ocean.

"Joshua," she cried out to her husband, "I didn't know the waves would come so far ashore. I thought we were safe."

He thrashed her again. "You are not fit to be a mother." Another lash of the whip. "Not fit! Not fit!"

"Joshua. Please. I tried to hold on to him. I tried." How could her husband doubt her? She thought she was the best mother in the settlement – perhaps the best in the world.

"You are wicked, Amanda." She cowered on the bed, her arms over her head as her husband in a fierce rage lashed the whip across her back and shoulders again and again.

"The Lord will never forgive you, Amanda. And neither will I," he shouted.

Next morning the surviving settlers buried all the dead bodies they could find and then gathered in makeshift pews amid the debris of their church for their regular Sunday service. Amanda sat with the congregation as her husband preached his sermon. He summarized his message by putting his hand on a makeshift cross that was propped beside him and in his best Puritan tone quoted a Proverb of Solomon: "Treasures of wickedness profit nothing. But righteousness delivereth from death. The Lord will not suffer the soul of righteousness to famish; but he casteth away the substance of the wicked."

Then he led them in a prayer for the souls of those lost to the storm.

Amanda stayed in her pew long after the service ended while the others gathered in small groups to discuss whether they should start rebuilding their homes on the Sabbath. The preacher finally pronounced they should not. Instead, they should spend the whole day in prayer. He would visit each family with instructions and with answers to their questions. That suited Amanda well. With her husband so occupied, she could be alone with the pain of the whipping, and with her guilt, her tears, and her loss of position. As the preacher's wife and the most devout example she could be, she had thought she was the most important woman in the settlement, a good two steps above all the others. How could this disaster have happened to her?

During the weeks following the hurricane, the settlers cleaned up the jumble of broken walls and driftwood and uprooted trees, salvaged what they could of their crops, and gathered berries and roots against the coming winter. Amanda worked hard with her neighbors but spoke little to anyone, so absorbed was she in her mind's struggle. And they had little to say to her, knowing her husband's judgement of her. Gone was her pride of place; gone was her haughtiness; gone was her leading position in the settlement. Her husband ignored her except to demand his meals be hot and on time, no matter they had meager food supplies and still had no proper house. She obeyed wordlessly.

By the time the leaves turned, though, Aiya's influence on Amanda was taking a stronger hold. In her times of silence and when she prayed for relief from her unbearable emotional distress, she registered higher and higher frequencies of Aiya's vibration. The effect was that she emerged slowly from the depths of her grief and began to find her inner center. Her mind strengthened and took command of itself. She cried less, her confidence returned, her mood brightened, her eyes cleared and she could smile when she watched children playing. And she exhibited a humility which was new to her.

It didn't matter that her husband's anger had faded not at all. It didn't matter that she was still shunned by some in the settlement who accepted her husband's assessment of her. It didn't matter even that her own brother kept his distance. Her sense of self came from within now, not from the voices of others. Memories of her son still brought her moments of grief but the guilt was gone; her pain was more for others now, not for herself.

Her husband had made her a separate bed, saying he could not trust her to have more children. Without a family of her own to care for she spent many hours helping her neighbors. Most of her neighbors now welcomed her bright energy into their lives in spite of her husband's continuing condemnation of her.

She became extremely close to one neighbor in particular, a woman whose children she helped care for. The two were like sisters, and were able to confide in one another about the most intimate details of their lives. "It sounds terrible to say it, but these many months since The Storm have been a blessing to me," Amanda confessed. "It has been like coming out of the darkness - like a rebirth. It is as though I have started a new life. I have never been so content. Life has become quite beautiful – even midst all the troubles we are having. I live with such ease."

As Aiya's love aspect stirred in Amanda's heart, she held all of her neighbors in a radiation of warmth and peacefulness which eased their pain and lifted their spirits. "Your heart is broken, dear sister," she would say quietly to a young widow, "and your children miss their father. Now, all of us are your family, your children are our children, and we are all in God's loving embrace. His love and ours will keep you safe."

For the rest of her life, Amanda and her husband spoke not a word to one another, except for his orders to her about meals and household chores. Nevertheless, she went to church with all the others in the settlement, attended bible readings and followed all her husband's religious rituals in their home. However, none of the outer trappings nor the blind dogma of her husband's church penetrated her heart. The simple underlying New Testament message of love was all she lived.

In the evenings, she went for long walks along the shore. At night, her dreams were of her own inner cathedral and of her own inner religion. Her prayers were that she might become an instrument of God's love. With each of those invocations, Aiya's presence shone more brightly in her consciousness.

As the years went by, though, the heavy work of the settlement's struggle for survival and her husband's overbearing negativity wore her down. It was a constant challenge for her to hold steady in the sweetness of spirit she had uncovered in herself. Moreover, her increased sensitivity to higher vibrations was more than her physical constitution could handle and the excessive stimulation of her body took its toll. It was an imbalance Aiya would have to address in a future incarnation.

Throughout her thirties, she suffered frequent illnesses which left her progressively weaker until, on her fortieth birthday, her heart gave out. She was buried in the churchyard cemetery which by then had more occupants than had the houses in the settlement.

Chapter Nine

The Entrepreneur

The cab driver murmured a throaty command to his horse as he pulled to a halt in front of the elegant gray stone house, one of a dozen on the finest block of Glasgow's finest street. From within the cab, a plume-hatted young lady pushed open the door, gathered her full skirts and put one foot out onto the low step. A passing gentleman glanced appreciatively at the booted ankle showing under the skirt and stepped quickly to her side, doffing his tall hat and putting his hand under her elbow as she stepped down. As she let go of her skirts, she smiled modestly and thanked him, then walked briskly across the sidewalk and up the five steps to the black and brass door.

Before she even touched the door handle, a servant in a black dress and white apron opened the door from the inside and dipped her head as the lady entered. The servant took her wrap and her hat and told her there would be tea in the conservatory straight away. The young lady nodded cursorily, turned her back and proceeded down the wide hall to the back of the house.

As she did so, she glanced through an open door into the parlor where her father was holding a meeting with ten or twelve dark-suited men with serious looks on their faces. It is probably something about getting a Scottish parliament, she thought, or maybe the building and financing of trading ships to the Far East. Perhaps it was his engineering friends discussing their canal project in Sweden. The early nineteenth century was alive with many industrial opportunities and her father had many interests. She averted her eyes and proceeded quickly past the door - her father could not abide interruptions or even momentary distractions.

The brief sight of the beautiful young lass did, however, distract one of the dark suits sitting in the parlor. He was Hamish Sinclair, a newly minted engineer and an extremely good-looking bachelor, according to the ladies of his acquaintance. He was in her father's meeting with his own father, a well-known Glasgow accountant. The topic was the British colony of Canada in North America and the new commercial opportunities arising, especially now that the invasion by the independent American states had been beaten back and the fur trade had pushed well into the west. The engineer was a bright and energetic young Scot looking for adventure and for wealth in his own right. Aiya was his soul, the inner being which the young man was vaguely starting to recognize as that certain something within that held the truth of life.

Aiya's many human experiences had shaped and strengthened its ability to hold steady its presence in the actions of its outer appearance – the personality. Each experience showed as a stronger personality than the previous one - a quieter emotional expression, a more clarified mental capacity, a more integrated personal will - leading to a finer sensitivity to soul's higher frequency vibrations. The Hamish Sinclair venture, however, needed to bring still more strengthening of the personality in order to stand an even higher voltage blast in the furnace of the soul's refining vibration.

Aiya's mastery of form had reached a point where its inhabitation of the engineer promised to be a campaign which would engender a deep mining of the personality's heart center in order to reveal its true potential to express the powerful love of soul.

Hamish was a crucial incarnation for Aiya. If successful, it would set the stage for the next incarnation which was on stream for the year 2005. That next experience would be the climax of Aiya's long march to freedom. It would be Aiya's finishing school - the time for the neutralizing of the last currents of personal self-concern. It would be the time, finally, for soul to secure a complete hold on the personality, the time when personality's will would take second place to soul's will in the life of a human. It would be the turning point when the personality would surrender completely to soul's impression, saying, once and for all, "Thy will, not my will."

Success with Hamish would depend on Aiya's ability to animate the consciousness of love so that it shone brightly in the personality's expression. Despite the fact that the Hamish personality was already quite strong, it would take the soul a few years to bring even more stability to the emotional body, an essential condition before Aiya could subject the man's system to the purifying frequency the campaign required.

As soon as the parlor meeting adjourned, the engineer excused himself to his father and the host, slipped out of the parlor and hurried down the hall, not sure where he would find his quarry but determined to do so. And he did.

Hamish Sinclair was a persuasive suitor and the courtship was brief. The marriage attracted wide attention – the beautiful daughter of Glasgow's finest and wealthiest gentleman and the handsome, dashing man-about-town. Hamish had only a few weeks with his bride before he boarded the four masted sailing ship for the colonial center of Montreal – a long enough honeymoon to start a family, not long enough, however, to know how she would manage during his absence.

He returned just in time for the birth of his son, bringing with him from the colony a trunk full of exotic gifts, a string of exciting tales of wealth, and endless heroic stories of hardship and suffering in the cold Canadian winter. He hardly had time to see his wife and infant son while he met with investors and made preparations to leave again. His wife had all the servants she needed, he reasoned, so she and the child would be well cared for while he was away making his fortune.

On his next return to Glasgow, Hamish found a son who was walking and a wife who was fully occupied with her society friends. They spent a few hours together and then went their separate ways again – he to his investors, she to her afternoon excursions and her teas and her theatre evenings.

Once more Hamish sailed across the Atlantic and plunged into his several business projects. He was gaining a reputation as a brilliant engineer and a man of action who could build a gristmill or a bridge or a wharf better and faster than anyone else. Investors were paying unprecedented fees to persuade him to head up their projects. He in turn was investing most of these payments in other enterprises in the colony. He was amassing a fortune which already far exceeded his dreams. A personable, strong-minded, action-oriented young man, he had become one of the leaders of the colony.

This time he was away for almost two years. When he returned, it was to a wife with a fourteen-month-old daughter and a three-year-old son. The children, of course, didn't recognize him as he disembarked the ship, and neither did his wife until he was within a few feet of them.

"My daughter is no wallflower, Hamish Sinclair," his father-in-law warned. "Agnes can't wait for you forever. She needs a husband in fact, not just in name. When are you going to be staying at home?"

"Aye, sir. I know it must be hard for her. But right now there is so much opportunity, so much money to be made. It would be a shame not to take advantage."

"And what about the children?"

"But sir, it is for Agnes and the children that I make these terrible voyages across the Atlantic. It is for them that I work as hard as I do and put up with that primitive colonial life. It is for them. So they will have whatever they want. I am doing all this for my family."

"You have no family, Hamish. You pay their keep but you no longer have any claim on them."

On the ship back to Montreal, Hamish thought about his father-in-law's statement – 'you have no family.' *What nonsense. They are mine. My wife. My children. They live in My house. I give them everything. They will not need her father's money. Not when I am slaving to give them the best life they could ever have. How could he say I have no family?*

Just two more years, he thought, *and I will have enough. Two more years and I will finish with Canada. Then home. Home? Think, Hamish, what is home? Glasgow? Sit around in a stuffy office? Drink whiskey at the club. Attend parties with your wife's friends? Is that what home means?*

It isn't so bad in Montreal, is it Hamish old man? People do things there. Interesting things. Big country things. And it seems to be mostly Scots who are running the place. Yes, we had a small people's rebellion, but that just made things interesting – another challenge. Even the weather is not bad when you are used to it. You feel alive there. And look at what you have accomplished. The best builder in the colony, they say, and none can disagree. Thirty-five years old and you can have any piece of work you want. For any price you ask. And now that we are shipping lumber back to Britain, your purse is growing like the virgin forest. He wished for stronger winds so the ship would sail faster. He looked forward to being back to work in Montreal with his friends.

Just two years later, as he was preparing for his return to Scotland, the letter arrived from Agnes. He had indeed decided to leave Montreal for the last time and return to settle in Glasgow. In these last two years their correspondence had been even less frequent than in his previous sojourns – her last letter had been six months ago. He interrupted his packing and looked at the front and back of the thin envelope, held it up to the light, weighed it in his hand, as though examining it would tell him the contents. Finally, he slit the seal and took out the single page. He unfolded it warily. "My dear Hamish," he read. "When you return to Glasgow, we will be gone." That was it. No explanation. It was signed, simply, "Agnes." Her father was right. He had no family.

The trip home seemed to take forever, and he didn't mind. Once home, he walked ceaselessly around Glasgow's streets, muttering to himself, his rumbling thoughts dragging him down deeper and deeper into despair. He stopped in to see his father-in-law who refrained from saying 'I told you so.' Rather, he let Hamish talk – and talk. When the words ceased to flow, the older man put his hand on his son-in-law's shoulder and said, "It takes time, Hamish. When your world falls apart, it takes time to decide how to make it whole again. It would be good for you to get away and spend some time on your own."

"Get away? I *have* been away. Where do you think I should go?"

"Somewhere different – entirely on your own - where new thoughts can germinate. Where you can see the world with fresh eyes. Like the Alps, for example. Why don't you go hiking in the Alps?"

It was a cloudy day in Geneva. Hamish stared into the dark patterns in the water of the Rhône River as it eased slowly out of Lac Léman and passed under the bridge that led to the farms along the side of the lake. He had arrived the day before and planned to spend a month hiking in the Alps, hoping to recover from the depression he had suffered since receiving the letter from Agnes. It turned out that Agnes and the children – three of them now - had gone to Australia with a teacher from the school his older son had been attending. The teacher would be Headmaster at a new school for boys in Sydney. They had been seeing one another in Glasgow for more than a year.

"Courage, Monsieur Sinclair," his hiking guide had said when he first met him. "Maybe tomorrow will be a better day." *Was he talking about the rainy weather,* Hamish wondered, *or my life. How can my life be better tomorrow? It's a wreck. My wife is gone. My children – they don't even know who I am. One of them I have never seen. I did everything for them. How could she?*

The dark water under the bridge absorbed him as he turned the questions over and over in his mind, rationality trying to find its way out of depression. His gut ached. His eyes swelled in tears. His whole body shook. "I came back!" he shouted at the river. "I came back. And you weren't there. You weren't there! Why weren't you there? Why?" The river didn't answer.

Next morning, the guide paused on the path at the top of the high pasture, puffed easily on his pipe, and pointed out features of the village in the valley below. Hamish could pick out the pension he had rented for the week. This first day they would just stroll through the high pastures. The same tomorrow. Gradually, as his legs became accustomed to climbing, they would go higher and farther, even do a little work with the ropes, perhaps.

He enjoyed being with the middle-aged Swiss. He enjoyed his smile, his relaxed manner, his quiet confidence in himself, and his peaceful coexistence with the world around him. He enjoyed the guide's stories of climbing expeditions. Woven into the stories was the man's simple philosophy about life: he lived in harmony with his mountains; he loved the beautiful life he had been given; he believed in a loving God who was with him wherever he went. In the aura of the guide's peaceful presence, Hamish could feel the cloud over his life beginning to lift, the miasma of his self-pity beginning to disperse. As his emotional noise subsided, it made room for the sound of soul.

On the fourth day, Hamish was in a much lighter mood as they set out from the village. His step was livelier, his eyes were brighter, his energy level was higher. Aiya's vibrance was getting through. The guide noted the change. "You had a good sleep, Mr. Sinclair?"

"I slept well, thank you. The village is quiet at night. The air is pure."

After two hours of steady climbing, Hamish stopped and took in the view of the surrounding mountain peaks. "I feel at home here," he said to the guide. "I seem to know these mountains – as though I have been here before." The guide smiled. It was always a pleasure to watch the mountains capture visitors. He noticed, though, that this man seemed genuinely to belong.

After each day's hike, Hamish sat on the broad porch of the chalet, watching the sun disappear behind the mountains and brooding on the questions of his life. In some of these quiet interludes, Aiya's brightened presence penetrated the energy field of his instrument with a more refined vibration. In response, the Hamish mind opened to a broader scope of intelligence that introduced a series of deeper questions.

So, Hamish, you are thirty-seven years old. Are you a success? You have wealth, power to get things done, a fine professional reputation, many friends. Is that success? Your marriage failed – does that make you a failure as a human being? Did your business success produce your marriage failure? What are the standards of success, Hamish? By the way, who sets your standards?

No easy answers emerged as the inklings of new truths, which were inherent in the questions, confronted old patterns of thought. Hamish put the questions aside. He relaxed and became lost in the magnificence of the sunset, feeling part of the natural world around him. He listened to the last chattering of the birds at dusk. He dwelt, then, in the silence of the arriving night.

In the quiet, in the dark, a glint of clarity touched his consciousness. *Okay, Hamish, what do you think is the definition of success? You don't know, do you? You have been running to the sound of an external trumpet, haven't you? Truthfully now, who was to blame for your separation from your family? Was it really Agnes? Was she the one who ran out? Or was it you? Didn't you constantly run out - to Montreal?*

He did not like the sharp knife of reality. His emotions took over. *But she went with another man. Why shouldn't I be angry? Was she so fed up with me being away that she had to find some one else? Was it spite? Did she have no loyalty? Did she have to take the children?* It was hard to hold the clarity, a classic case of the battle between reality and illusion. Aiya's pressing influence was on the side of reality. The personality clung to illusion.

His conversations with himself stopped short of answers – short of making explicit the answers he was afraid were lurking deep within. To be continued, he would say to himself. Let it simmer in the back of the mind.

In the third week, in their third village, Hamish asked his guide to allow him to hike on his own – he thought he needed some time alone. The guide simply puffed his pipe and nodded.

Hamish left the valley and climbed the mountains high above the village, above the alpine meadows where the farmers grazed their cows in the summer, above the tree line to the bare ridges and sheer rock faces which rose cleanly into the sky. He found a comfortable ledge where he sat in the warm sun. He relaxed and set free the questions which poured through his head when he was on the valley floor, setting them free in the royal halls of these majestic mountains where they evolved and matured. And where new questions were born in the far reaches of his mind, and new answers appeared.

Here, in the rarified silence of the mountains, the mind of Aiya's instrument became still enough to resonate with a very high soul frequency. As it resonated and then merged with that high frequency, it lost the boundaries of its individuality and registered a sense of being in infinite space. Hamish picked up the registration in his conscious awareness and was in awe. He resisted the natural urge of the lower mind to make concrete sense of the abstract condition, instead staying with the unnatural experience of being in space.

The confusion and the anger and the blame had no life in the infinite. Aiya's influence had brought another level of purity to the emotional and mental bodies, giving a finer clarity and a capacity for a deeper probing of the issues of his life. Hamish let the silence of the mountains open the portals of knowing. Simple truths emerged from the abstract space.

Something else emerged from the space. Not a question. Not an answer. Rather, a new consciousness - a new realization. Something beyond questions and answers. Something greater, but Hamish knew not quite what it was. He waited.

A breeze of awareness blew through him, and now he knew what it was. It was the infinite. Something about the infinite. *Yes, the infinite – I am in the infinite. No – I am the infinite. That's it. It is what the mystics have said. I am no longer just Hamish Sinclair – I am the infinite life of the universe. I am the sun and the moon and the stars. I am the mountains and the trees, the rocks and the heather. I am the birds. I am the animals.* He felt he was physically blending, integrating, interpenetrating at the atomic level, with all of his surroundings. *The infinite I am and always would be, now and forevermore.*

His spirit soared without limit, high above the peaks. With that opening, another filament of Aiya's life aspect touched Hamish's heart and initiated a bright vibration which passed through the whole of the instrument's body. At that moment, Hamish recognized, absolutely, he was Aiya. "I am soul," he murmured. "In the first place, I am soul." He was startled and overawed by his discovery. He had not expected this from what he had learned in the Scottish church. His recognition of the fact of soul filtered through his mind. Calm prevailed. He knew peace, a peace unlike any he had ever known before. Time stood still.

As he soaked in the quiet, he became aware of a hawk circling just below him, riding the thermal updraft. He followed the spirals of the hawk's path, upward, upward, until it hovered at his eye level. The up close sight of the hawk brought him back to his Hamish consciousness. "Take hold of yourself, Hamish," he said aloud. "Come down to earth." He had to look at his hands and feet and the rocks around him to assure himself he was not dreaming. It was no dream. Absorbing the reality of his experience and the true knowing of his thoughts, he laughed with pleasure. He stood up and spread his arms, joining with the wind and the hawk and with life itself. He gave an exuberant shout to the soaring bird, "We fly together, oh Great Spirit. We are one and the same, you and I." Then to himself, "Yes, we are one. One we are. One I am. I am."

He stood motionless, lost in reverence for the life he had discovered, lost in timeless space. Then he decided. He would leave the mountains immediately and return to Scotland. It was time to get on with what he had to do. He brushed the dust off his tweed trousers, slung his small packsack over his shoulder, turned to give a last wave to the disappearing hawk, and started back down the rocky trail.

In Glasgow, he went straight to his father-in-law and stated, "I am going to Australia, sir. I want her back."

"Wait, Hamish. My daughter and grandchildren will be home soon. Her Headmaster is a bore. Just wait."

He was right. She arrived home within the month. Her father invited Hamish to tea, and she was there waiting for him.

"Hamish, I am very glad to see you. Are you well?"

"Well enough. And you? And the children? Australia seems to have agreed with you."

"We enjoyed the sunshine. It is very warm there."

"All right now, you two," said her father. "You have lots to talk about so I shall leave you be. Ellen will bring you tea."

"Hamish," Agnes began immediately, "do you want your old life – in Montreal. Or do you want us?" She could be very direct when she chose. It always brought him up short.

He thought he knew what he wanted – to create a loving family life. That was his mountain top decision. He was willing to go to Australia to make it happen. Now, though, when he faced her, he questioned his motive for wanting her back. *Do I want to be a family man? Family is a first order manifestation of the Oneness I have become. I long for a close relationship with my children. That much is clear. But do I really love Agnes? In fact, do I really know her? Do I want to live her lifestyle?*

It was not easy to bring the mountaintop down into the valley. Valley habits of thinking could overwhelm abstract mountaintop idealism. Rushing from a new recognition of universal love and oneness to an old familiar form - the well-rehearsed desire to retake his family - may have been too quick a translation. Now he wondered if it had been an appropriate translation.

The questions flowed rapidly. *Why did I want her back? Do I really want her back after she ran off with another man? Could I get past that scandalous indiscretion of hers? On the mountain it was easy to decide.* On the mountain, with the hawk, his heart soared with the love of life, with the love of every form of life's expression, with every living thing. Agnes, in her essential being, although not in her personality, was incorporated within that love.

He remembered the mountain experience and relived its quality as they sat together. He spoke firmly. "I have left Montreal for good, Agnes. Just as I said I would two years ago. I have retired. I am ready to settle here as a family." She nodded. It was done.

It turned out to be not much of a reconciliation, however. They slept in separate bedrooms, spoke to each other very seldom except about the children, and in social situations they acted coolly toward one another, albeit correctly. Agnes spent a lot of time visiting with her mother and socializing with her lady friends. They rarely entertained at home. Servants provided most of the care for the children.

Hamish had an office in the center of town where he managed his investments, but spent a lot of time reading in his library at home – Homer and other accounts of Greek mythology, poets like Blake and Wordsworth – things he missed in his engineering education. He also delved into the New Testament in a way he hadn't done in church classes as a youth. He read the biography of St. Francis of Assisi and writings by Buddhist and Indian mystics. He found he was able to grasp abstract thought far more deeply than before and to bring it down to his concrete, practical mind.

Inevitably, after three years, Agnes and Hamish divorced. Hamish moved to his club in town. Agnes and the children stayed in the house. Curiously enough, he met with the children at their football games and musical recitals and school affairs more often than during the time they had lived together. He took them on special outings almost every weekend. They told him how much they enjoyed being with him. They had serious discussions together and they laughed a lot. The children agreed that he was more relaxed and more fun than any of their friends' fathers.

Nevertheless, after five years of retirement, he began to pay more and more attention to his financial interests in Montreal. He eventually concluded he could not remain an absentee investor, that he was needed on site. After all, he reasoned to a business friend, "I'm only forty-two years old and the businesses could use my drive as well as my engineering expertise." This time, however, he was truly torn between his children and Montreal. But again, Montreal won.

He could not believe the exciting changes which had taken place in the years he was away from the colony. The place was exploding with possibilities. He took up the challenges with enthusiasm and was soon deep into a new round of ventures, some of which took him west into Upper Canada, a whole new arena for his energies. However, the people who worked for him saw a new boss, one who was unique among his peers in that he seemed to care sincerely for the welfare of his employees. "They are human, my friend," he would say. "Therefore, I treat them that way. Aye, and it is just the way I would like to be treated." In those days, especially in the colonies, that was no small amount of caring.

On the ship back to Glasgow, he anticipated the pleasure of being once more with his three children. His heart sang as he tried to picture them. After two years they will certainly have grown, he mused. What kind of youngsters have they become? He couldn't wait to see.

"No sir, Mr. Sinclair. I am sorry. I have quite clear instructions. The children do not want to see you. Nor do madam and her husband. Now if you'll excuse me, sir, I must close the door."

Madam and her husband. Hamish returned to Canada and buried himself in work. His empire in the colony was growing mightily. He returned to Glasgow every two years and each time attempted to see his children. Each time he was rebuffed. Each time he returned to the colony with a new intensity for his work and an even higher level of care for his employees, a care he now extended to everyone he met. He had a new reputation: the kindest, most unselfish man in the colony. He was truly a changed person whose genuine concern for others had completely replaced his addiction to money and power.

On one of his visits back to Glasgow, Hamish received a message from an old school chum asking him to meet in the lounge of his club. As Hamish entered the lounge, there was a loud shout and a noisy drumroll. "Attention please gentlemen! Attention please. Here he is, once more back from the colonies." The voice was that of his school friend who was standing in front of the fireplace. "A toast, gentlemen. To the Conqueror!" About sixty men, Hamish's old school friends, financial partners and business acquaintances, raised their glasses in salute.

"To the Conqueror!" they chorused.

"Happy Fiftieth Birthday, Hamish Sinclair. And may your second fifty years be just as grand and glorious." His friend gave him a walloping slap on the back, put a whiskey in his hand, and began to sing an insulting barrack room song. The rest of the room immediately joined the affectionate chorus.

Next day at lunch, his school friend introduced him to three ladies sitting at a nearby table. "The one in the blue, Hamish," he said afterward behind his menu. "I saw how you looked at her, my friend. Her name is Fiona MacKenzie. She is a widow and the loveliest person you will ever meet."

"Indeed?"

"Yes, indeed. And you, my friend, you are the loveliest person she will ever meet. You are a new man, Hamish, not the calculating perpetual motion machine I used to know. You have become something of a saint, I fear, and you have come to deserve someone like Fiona. I mean that sincerely, my friend."

Between the lunch tables, Aiya and the soul of Fiona joined in resonance. "So, we meet once again, Ohruu," Aiya intoned.

"They don't know it now, Aiya, but your Hamish and my Fiona are in it for life."

Hamish and Fiona became close companions almost immediately. In the weeks after their meeting, they went to the theatre, they went for long walks, they met with friends for lunch, they sat quietly and talked, they laughed, they shared their most intimate thoughts. They connected as though they had always known and loved one another. "No need for a long courtship, Hamish," his school friend urged one day. "Get on with it."

Within a month, they had decided to get married as soon as Hamish returned from one last trip to

Canada to wind up his affairs. It was a surprise to both of them that they could make such a decision so soon and so easily. "And at our age, Hamish," Fiona laughed. "But I have not one thread of doubt, my love."

"Nor do I," He agreed. "I think ours will be a marriage made in heaven."

The day he arrived in Montreal on that final visit he took up his pen and wrote: "My Dearest Fiona, Our love has woven a bridge across the great ocean which lies between us, so I feel we are not separated. It is as though our two beings have become one."

The unifying love which Hamish had described in his letter was, in fact, the common vibration frequency which the Fiona and Hamish souls shared as members of the same soul group. The harmonization of their energies made the two personalities immediately feel as one.

It took Hamish five months to wind up all his affairs in the colony and turn everything into cash, credits, and fur pelts. During those five months, he sent a long letter to Fiona on every ship that left Montreal for Glasgow, and received as many from her.

Now, as he sailed home, he knew in these last few years he had discovered what it meant to be truly successful. "It has nothing to do with all the glamorous trappings of the material world," he had related to one of his Montreal merchant friends. How far he had come, he thought, since that first day on the bridge in Geneva. "No, indeed. Success is simply the ability to love – to love in the deepest sense. It has taken me all my life to discover that simple fact."

"Are you in dreamland, Sinclair? Have you lost your ambition, old man, to say nothing of your common sense?" the merchant chided him.

Hamish acknowledged the man's skepticism with a smile. He did not need to argue the point - his own inner serenity told him he was right. Love was everything. His ability to sustain the love quality in his daily affairs came from an inner voice that spoke to him frequently, not in words but in thoughts. He knew it was the voice of his mind's refined frequency resonating to the truth of soul.

He was conscious that it was in this deep way that he loved his employees and his treatment of them was an outward expression of a quality of soul that played in him ever more strongly. Like an echo, his love encouraged them to relate to others in a loving way. It was the same with his friends. He also knew how his love of his children had enlivened them in those few years he was close to them – and he was sure his love would be a magnet that would bring them close again - soon.

His love for Fiona had found a resonance that brought them quickly and wholly together. How simply, yet how deeply, they related to each other, how easily they integrated their lives; how few were the wrinkles as they achieved a smooth mutual understanding.

When he lived that pervasive love quality, he knew, all those around him could resonate in its peace. *Yes*, he affirmed to himself, *I know what success is.*

From the ship's rail, he scanned the crowds on the dock as the crew worked to secure the lines. When he spotted Fiona he cried out with delight - his three children were at the dock with her. He ran down the gangplank and threw his arms around them all.

The children had taken Fiona to their hearts and the three of them participated in the wedding party. Aiya and Ohruu vibrated brightly. "This marriage will be what marriages are supposed to be," the two souls agreed. "They will have a long and loving life together."

"Hamish, old man." The voice of his best man – his school chum - came with a wallop on the back.

"You son-of-a-gun, you've done it. You and your bride – you are the perfect couple. It must be the work of the gods, you saintly scoundrel."

Chapter 10

Soul's Review

"So, Aiya, how did you manage to get such a grip on the Hamish personality?"

"Ultimately, it was the silence of the mountains, Ohruu."

"Ah yes, the mountains."

Hamish and Fiona had passed on within a few months of one another. Now it was time for Aiya and Ohruu to absorb the lessons of their incarnations and weave the essential threads of meaning into the pattern of their eternal journeys, a pattern which incorporated the threads of all the learnings of all their previous human engagements. It was a pattern which, by stages, would blend with the design of our ultimate human destiny.

"It is not the first time the magic of the mountains created an invitation to expand the mind of my instrument. It happened when I took the form of the farmer who stopped the runaway. He and Hamish climbed the very same mountain, Ohruu, and sat on the same rock ledge."

Like others in their group, Aiya and Ohruu melded naturally with one another and each absorbed the other's thoughts easily. "Hamish was a breakthrough for my work, Ohruu, a quantum leap forward."

"It was marvelous, my friend. It set you up nicely for your final test coming up in your next journey into form."

"It was my previous three rounds, though, Ohruu, which were especially important in opening the door."

"The preacher's wife - after the hurricane?"

"Yes. She found her inner peace and her own higher authority after she heard my sounding and glimpsed the light of soul. Before that, the farmer. He opened his mind to the plane of pure reason. He had a first intuitive glimpse of another realm of reality. And before him, the pirate. That event gave us the first opening to the abstract plane of mind."

"The mountains, Aiya, don't forget the mountains."

"The mountains, yes. The mountains have such a clear vitality, yet such stillness, such space for our action. You know, Ohruu, how stubbornly humans can cling to their illusions."

"Indeed."

"In that rarified mountain energy, we can turn illusions to dust. We can break up those thoughts which imprison them and free the mind to see new possibilities. Then we can touch the mind with the fact of the infinite and awaken the heart to the life all-encompassing. Because of all the preparation in previous incarnations, the Hamish personality was ready."

"It was not an easy life, though, for your Hamish, Aiya. Your constant impulse pushed him to the extreme."

"To the very edge. The stronger, more aligned his personality, the more he responded to my pressure. The more he responded, the more his ambition grew – personal ambition was how the self-concerned personality interpreted the pressure of soul. Montreal was his siren – he could not resist the lure of wealth and power and the status it brought. Ultimately though, at the limit, the mindset hardened and started to crystallize. Eventually, of course, it shattered, and then the mind was open to the infinite."

"Ah, the old game of making it worse in order to make it better – a way to open the door to soul consciousness. The personality structure must have been very strong to resist as long as it did."

"Indeed it was, Ohruu. The pursuit of wealth and power was a fixation that was tough to break. Wealth and power gave the young Hamish his sense of identity in the world, so he hung on stubbornly."

"Of course, that strength was needed to handle the high frequency currents you later had to infuse."

"It's the paradox, isn't it. You build the strength of personality's will; then when it is strong enough to handle the higher frequencies, you force it to give up its will and surrender to soul's will."

"That's the Law."

"If only everyone knew it was the Law, our work could go so much more smoothly. For the very strong Hamish personality it was, inevitably, a battle. He struggled. He suffered. Always the resistance leads to suffering. Eventually, out of the challenges of his entrepreneurial work and the trauma of his marriage experience, he wrought a stability of his energy field, and its frequency rose by several octaves. The stepping up invoked the power of my will, which shattered the armor of personality's self-concern. He began to see he was more than the person of Hamish. Our love and light started to shine through."

"Was it immediate?"

"At first, it was intermittent."

"Old thought patterns take a while to disintegrate."

"Yes, he had to become familiar with the energy of a brighter expression. Quite quickly, though, his outer life began to reflect his inner more clearly and showed up as a kind and loving personality. We were on our way toward full integration."

"Your love aspect was in full bloom in the Hamish of later years. Your will, your love, your presence in his life – your life shone through the outer personality mask as brightly as a jewel."

"Hamish was a good instrument, Ohruu."

"And then you and I reconnected as Hamish and Fiona."

"A happy coincidence."

"Not entirely coincidence, Aiya."

"What do you mean?"

"As members of the same group, we have been tuning our mental frequencies to a common note. You know we operate on the same frequency and our connection is solid. Our tuners are not always on, but our antennae are always out and listening."

"True enough - as though they are locked on a homing signal."

"Exactly. As soon as Hamish and Fiona met, you and I attended to the resonance from our antennae and recognition was immediate."

"Then our harmonizing amplified a common energy vibration.

"The amplified energy attracted mental substance, and . . ."

"And the mental substance became a strong thought."

"Right. Form followed thought – the wedding was the externalization of what you might call our inner marriage."

The two souls drifted silently in the substance of their thoughts.

"Ah, Aiya, I see you are entering a state of intense concentration. You need the space to continue absorbing all the wisdom you can extract from your earth experience, so I'll withdraw for now."

Aiya held the focus of concentration. It was the winter interlude of the cycle following the gathering up the harvest. It was a time for separating the wheat from the chaff and examining the kernels. It had been an incarnation of great significance for Aiya, a difficult rite of passage along the path to freedom. There was much to absorb in this season in preparation for the next stage of the rhythmic cycle.

When the assembly of the Hamish learning had been completed, Aiya's attention entered the second part of the winter - a period of contemplation, integration and alignment with purpose. It was a time for taking stock of all the soul had learned, all it had become – to see itself as the product of all the lives that had gone before. It was a time for reorienting, for becoming aware of a new higher frequency of being, for seeing the implications of some new capacities, for clarifying and stabilizing the newly achieved status. It was a time of preparing for the breathing out, preparing for the spring planting of new seeds – preparing for the next incarnation.

In the normal soul condition of deep meditation, orientating to its higher source, Aiya was aware not only of the past and the present, but, simultaneously, the soul was aware of the future – it existed in timelessness. The soul's evolutionary status – that is, the level of refinement of its ability to express its vibration in the human form - reverberated in the chamber of the universal forces of perfection. Where there was imperfection in Aiya's tone, a dissonance sounded, the way an out-of-tune musical instrument offends an ear that hears with perfect pitch. The dissonance thus produced by the soul's remaining imperfections induced a tension which registered in Aiya's core. The interaction of this tension with the relentless pressure of the planet's evolutionary impulse produced, in turn, several demands to refinement which would resolve the dissonance. These demands formed the themes of action for Aiya's next incarnation. The themes took shape as streams of energy, like magnetic filaments, which created possible avenues of purpose for Aiya's next incarnation.

As the energy streams of Aiya's themes became more coherent, they were magnetically attracted to complementary themes generated by others in the group with whom Aiya had shared many lives. From among the possible themes, those which resonated most strongly within the group formed a coherent family of action streams which were a calling together of those who would incarnate in a harmony of mutual support around a common evolutionary purpose. And so, with the strength of their unity, the group's coherent streams of action would manifest as a new wave of human activity on earth.

A vibrant note in the coalescing group drew Aiya's focus, a note which became so loud Aiya could hear no others. It was the note sounded by a wave that incorporated intention, creation and exteriorization. It was the Love Impulse, which some called the Christ Impulse and others called by other names, such as Maitreya and Vishnu. It embraced the earth and rang true for Aiya like no other note. Why Aiya found it so dominant became clear as the soul saw others, like Ohruu, tuning to it with a similar exclusivity. This was the time for the Savior's return, Aiya realized, and all of those in Aiya's group, and many other groups, were being carried into human form on His wings.

"It will be our purpose, will it not Ohruu, to hold our alignment with the Christ Impulse so as to manifest its love in human form."

"Indeed Aiya – and in measure unlike our planet has ever before seen."

*Once upon a time there was a Prince for all the people
And a land for the Prince to rule.
But chaos raged in the land because
The people would not obey the Prince's laws.
So the Prince watched and waited.*

*The people were in disorder and distress
And prayed for salvation.
They prayed for the Prince
To return to the land and bring them peace.
The Prince watched and waited.*

*Then the people prayed for strength,
That they might serve the Prince
And obey his laws.
And they were heard.*

*The word went out:
The time is now; the Prince is on his throne,
His Kingdom is reclaimed.
The people rejoiced.*

Their peace had set them free.

The ancient parable spoke a truth to Aiya. People all over the world have been praying for the intervention of a Savior, a Mediator, an Avatar, whose name depended on the tradition from which they issued their prayers – names such as the Messiah, the Maitreya, the Imam Mahdi, the Christ. Their prayers gave voice to the unconscious urging impulse of their essential selves – their souls. As Ohruu had explained, "We urge our human forms forward toward finer living and their response is to pray for external intervention to bring them that finer living. They miss the point. They think their salvation comes from outside.

"Soon, though, they will know us, their souls, to be that inner reality, the essence of each individual, the immortal entity, the spark which has long been hidden from human awareness by the personality's attachment to the human form. When finally they know us, they will look from within for the answer to their yearning.

"Some of us have been able to break through the density of the form and have begun to be present enough to express our purpose through the mask of personality. The awareness shown by your last instrument, Aiya, the engineer Hamish, demonstrated you have succeeded in that endeavor well beyond the norm for today's humanity. I think my Fiona showed equal awareness.

"In time, many more souls will be able to shine their qualities through the human form. Then people will realize their own responsibility for their salvation instead of calling to external saviors. When enough people have created their own peace – within themselves and with each other – then the Savior will come to build on their vibration of peace and create a new world."

Chapter Eleven

Soul's Journey

"Listen, Ohruu. There are new harmonics in our energy fields."

"Since our Hamish and Fiona times, Aiya, we have been sounding another frequency. It means a new capacity for expression." The two souls were discussing what their winter interlude of concentration had revealed and how their new condition might play in their next incarnations.

"I hear a richer resonance too."

"That means we'll have more strength for our next sojourn in human form."

"I can hardly believe our journey is almost over, Ohruu. How long ago did it begin?"

"Aeons, my friend. Before there were records. At least, before the records you and I can read." Ohruu had spent many form-lives as an Asian and was something of an expert on what was called the Ancient Wisdom. Those embodiments had produced a patient, absorptive, contemplative entity who had delved deeply into the history of humanity. Ohruu knew, for example, about the collective karma of earth's sixty billion entities that were cycling through human forms, currently at the rate of some six billion at a time.

"You and I first incarnated among the earliest inhabitants of the earth," Ohruu said as he retrieved their distant past. "We go back to the days of primitive beings, barely distinguishable from the animals with which we competed for survival. The mentality of humans then was nearly non-existent. Physical survival was everything and, like animals, humans were driven by instinct. They gathered in clusters for mutual protection, just like the animals. No one dared wander away from the herd lest they fall prey to animals or other human herds that were competing for food. They knew themselves only as the band or the tribe, a cluster of blood related family members.

"The journey for humans has been long and arduous. When one band became stronger or bigger, it could take what it wanted from other bands, each ready to kill before being killed. Life was violence, Aiya.

"Then some among the tribes showed more skill than others, some were more forceful in their demands than others. They seemed to have ideas the rest of the tribe didn't have, ideas beyond their usual animal instincts. Sometimes their tribes rejected them. Sometimes they emerged as leaders, not like the alpha wolf, relying on instinct. These leaders were somehow quite different. They were part of the tribe yet their bearing made them somehow separate, as though they knew something the rest didn't know. The souls of these leaders learned to animate the germ of self, and thus the human family began its conscious struggle to grow as individuals."

"My Headman's Woman," Aiya recalled.

"Exactly. As individuals gradually broke away from tribal consciousness, they emerged from the darkness of anonymity into the first light of individuality. As they awoke, they discovered a new idea – the concept of self – and it became a preoccupation. They identified the self by identifying what was not the self. With little inner awareness, they looked outward to the reactions of others to know themselves. They showed their individuality by marking themselves distinctly and wearing ornaments, and by striving for preferred positions in the social structure. As the germ of self grew, they sought to grow in self-importance and they did that by striving for power over those around them.

"They couldn't control their natural environment, however. It was still their master. What they could not comprehend, they attributed to the work of the gods who were all-powerful and not to be displeased, for they would wreck havoc on offenders. They noted the cycles of the heavens, of the seasons, of human life, and they created mythologies to explain how the world worked. They invented rituals to align themselves with the unseen forces, and they struggled to know their place as humans.

"Gradually, over the aeons, incarnation by incarnation, as their unsophisticated human minds slowly registered the spark of the evolutionary impulse, their desire for selfhood strengthened. In the only way they could then imagine, they turned to the material world around them. As individuals, they began to own things. To satisfy their desires, they took what they could for themselves, fighting for what they wanted, stealing, lying, killing, raping - now in the name of enhancing the perception of self rather than out of an instinctual urge for tribal survival. They solidified their illusion of self by husbanding and reveling in their material possessions.

"Eventually the fires of desire became too much for their feeble minds. In their greed and physical excesses, they became so destructive they could not go on. Their evolutionary march was in a cul-de-sac. They had either to abandon what their desires had produced, abandon how they had defined the self, or else give up their place in the evolutionary queue. It would take a new mentality to save them.

"Humanity's need was answered by the incarnation of a line of more mentally developed leaders, first in India, then in Egypt. Their ideas were seminal. They led people to reach beyond their physical selves for strength, to reach to heaven to know who they were. Later, in Greece, advanced thinkers inspired people to reach into higher levels of the mind for new ways of thinking, feeling and acting. Under their influence, people began to change their ideas about self and society, they learned to turn their minds inward and think for themselves, and they learned to think new thoughts.

"People's desires were still strong, their mental fields were still rough and still overgrown with emotional distortion, but the seeds of advanced mental development had been planted. The first roots of Western civilization, as we now know it, took hold. Now people had a mental sensitivity which began to register some of the refined impressions coming from beyond the physical world."

"And the people could then consciously register the vibration of God?" Aiya asked. "They had that potential?"

"Some had that potential. At first just a few were able to respond and then only a little. In time, more people found the touch. A few groups of sensitives came together as prophets and teachers. Their work amplified the vibration."

"And then later," Aiya posited, "the Love Impulse, or the Christ Impulse as some call it, which had been approaching from a distance, came to earth in a physical form."

"Yes, the Christ manifested the impulse of love by overshadowing a human form for just a few years in the life of that great servant called Jesus of Nazareth. And the message was clear: humanity's only way forward, the only way for humans to rise to their potential, was to respond to that universal impulse of love, to register it in their human minds and hearts so it would inspire them in their actions. The Impulse would help humans know their oneness – with one another, and with all that is."

"And how much have humans absorbed that message in these last two thousand years, Ohruu? We still see people seeking a separative individuality by ornamenting themselves, husbanding material possessions, and seeking power over others. People still steal, lie, kill and rape to get what they want."

"How true. There are many who have yet to get through that stage. Nevertheless, Aiya, humanity has come a long way, uneven though the progress has been."

"But there is so much disorder in the world, Ohruu. You have to question our progress."

"You are right about the disorder, Aiya. However, look at the other side – at the order that is in fact emerging. The world is coming together in many ways – the oneness of humanity is starting to show. Many developments during the fifty years since the Second World War demonstrate that progress. Think of the economic and political unions of countries that, not long ago, were at war. Think of the growing ideal of democracy in Latin America, Eastern Europe and elsewhere, the many international organizations for all kinds of constructive purposes, the international programs of aid. There have been so many changes toward oneness, Aiya. People now act compassionately beyond their own country borders, across oceans, across differences in race, color and religion. One World is becoming a reality, not just an idealistic phrase."

"I suppose it does show at the international level."

"Not only internationally. There are also huge changes within countries and within communities, Aiya. In many countries there are comprehensive government and volunteer social programs, compassionate work among the sick and the poor, a concern for human rights, a concern for the environment. People are showing respect for all life on the planet, in whatever form or species it manifests.

"And look, Aiya, at the thousands of goups gathering for peace – speaking peace, singing peace, meditating peace.

"In the history of humanity, these are all recent ideas, Aiya. People's thoughts became much more orderly after the fires of the World War helped clear the mental plane of humanity. It was at the same time a great tragedy, of course, that humanity was unable to muster the strength of will to achieve the same clarity without so much devastation. Nevertheless, humanity is moving on, influenced by a new breed of leaders in all parts of the world.

"The twentieth century brought a new energy into the world, a new level of quality backed by strong forces pressing our evolution forward. In the twenty-first century, the pressure is accelerating. The peace movement is gathering strength in the minds of a very wide community of concerned and active participants. Perhaps most remarkably, wars are now considered obsolete by many of the world's major powers, notwithstanding a few notable exceptions.

"The old order is collapsing under the pressure. Old doctrines and old institutions are becoming irrelevant for the new condition – they no longer give satisfactory answers. Tradition is losing its hold. There is a new openness in seeking solutions and a new urgency to move forward."

"But what about all those people who are still behaving in the old ways."

"Aiya, even those behaviors which seem contrary to the new impulse are evidence humanity is moving ahead. People who are unable to see a positive vision of the future become frightened by the changes. The forces which are impulsing the planet are shaking the foundations of their values and beliefs, challenging their sense of identity. They feel threatened, they fear losing what they have, they fear losing their way. They look for safety and comfort in their religious, ethnic, or tribal identities, and in the certainty of rigid dogma. As they face what they perceive to be the danger of change, they cling more firmly to their old familiar ways, often embracing the extremes of their old institutions and rituals.

"Paradoxically, these conservative voices are a valuable contribution to progress. When they become loud enough, they reveal more clearly how their positions are inappropriate to the new conditions, and thus they highlight more clearly what has to change. Sometimes we have to have more darkness in order to be aware of the light. Conservative voices also act as a screen that sifts the useful new ideas from the not so useful. That helps the implementation of change.

"In time though, as the unrelenting pressure of the forward impulse increases, the defenders of the past become strident, even fanatical, in the face of the deep inner impulse toward a New World. Their positions get more rigid as they try to resist. Their defenses harden. Eventually, inevitably, their positions become brittle, they crystallize, and then they shatter."

"When you put it that way, Ohruu, it becomes clear that what we perceive as positive and negative forces actually work together as one movement along the forward path."

"You know the story, Aiya. When the old ways of thinking die, the Prince will rule again. The world will rejoice. The healing force of the Logos is ever ready to respond, waiting only for us to clear away humanity's old orientations, waiting for us to achieve a sufficient refinement of our instruments for the New Kingdom to take root."

"When the old ways of thinking die . . . But when?"

"It will happen. Believe it, Aiya. The forces for change are irresistible. They are pressing forward, no matter what."

Aiya thought about their coming incarnations. "We will be part of that force, Ohruu. That will be our work."

"Yes, that will be our work. The landing of the new round of the Love Impulse needs fertile ground. We must make sure we do our part to help prepare the way."

"It will mean a new mentality will be brought to the affairs of the world."

"Some people are so equipped already, Aiya. They are the true leaders.

"I hope to be among such people in this coming round."

"You may well be. I see you beginning to resonate with that young couple in London, Aiya. Perhaps they will provide you with your next human form."

"They are Eva and Ian Cameron. They could be the parents. They are expecting a son in August 2005 – just six months from now."

"Eva and Ian are among the new leaders who have begun to manifest our new Love Impulse."

"Their light shows brightly, doesn't it. It is a very fine quality of energy that radiates and attracts others to our common work. They give a lot of their time to African relief programs, inspired by their deep love for humanity."

"You have chosen well, Aiya. Their alignment with the Impulse will be a good example to their son."

"There is also a family heritage of service, Ohruu. Ian's father and grandfather, and both of Eva's parents are living examples of service to humanity. They will immerse their child in their strong social values. And the athletic ability of the two parents promises their child will have a genetic heritage of physical vigor."

"If that is your path, Aiya, your vehicle should have a good start in life."

"I think the work would thrive."

"If you could bring to the child's genetic heritage your advanced soul heritage – the capacity you have developed for handling the form world - there is a high probability your expression of the Love Impulse would be a magnificent contribution. It is fair to expect, Aiya, if you become the newest Cameron, you will be one of the leaders the world will remember when the history of the twenty-first century is written."

"If that happens, Ohruu, it will be a very different life than the one lived by the child's nineteenth century ancestor. The great great great grandfather, Harry Cameron, was no shining example to the community."

Aiya tuned to the historical records of the Cameron family he hoped to join and opened the book on Harry Cameron.

Chapter Twelve

Harry Cameron and Young Harry

"Is he dead, Jock? Look. He's nae movin.' Ye better check."

The constable unlocked the cell door and the two men went in and bent over the hulk lying crumpled on the rough stone floor. Together they heaved the prisoner on to his back.

"Oh dear God." They shrank from the corpse. Its lifeless eyes stared up at them.

"Ach, poor Harry Cameron. He'll nae get drunk again."

"Now w'at's to become o' that young family o' his?"

"It'll be the poor house for 'em - 'e'll leave 'em nuthin'."

"Aye. And them wee bairn - are they gonna come to no good, like their father?"

"Like as not. That young lad o' theirs – Young Harry – he's already adrift."

"Aye. Like father, like son."

It was a miserably wet morning as the horse-drawn funeral wagon led a small cluster of mourners to the churchyard cemetery. Harry's wife, Agnes, walked with her year old daughter in her arms. She bent her head in proper mourning, keeping her eyes on the road and her face well obscured by a large black shawl. Her six-year-old son, Young Harry, walked straight and tall with a new maturity in his eyes. He led his two little sisters by the hand. Four uncles and aunts and an array of cousins shuffled along behind. The villagers lined the streets as they went by, shaking their heads and muttering quiet curses at the dead father. The men tipped their hats to the widow.

Harry Cameron had been the village bully. A huge man, he regularly lashed out with his iron fists, swearing blue clouds of vile curses, blindly abusing whomever he saw as a ready victim. When he went too far, as he often did, a gang of townsmen would take him on and drag him away. His drinking made him even worse, fuelling his belligerence and sending him into bloody brawls, which he seemed to relish, until the gang beat him into the ground. Every Friday night, on schedule, the jail cell floor was his bed.

His wife looked forward to Friday nights for it was the only night she could count on not getting a beating. It was probably the beatings which led to the malformed body of their first son who had died within days of his birth. Now, if she would admit it, she would say her husband's death was a blessing. In fact she had often, after a beating, silently wished he were dead, never believing it would ever happen of course. As she huddled with her children under the tree by the grave, there were no tears on her cheeks.

Although they suffered the sights and sounds of his rage, their father never physically struck the children. The girls he ignored and Young Harry he enrolled in his bully bravado view of the world.

"See now, Young Harry," he would say, "never let anyone cast a sideways look at ye. Show 'em yu're just as gud as anyone."

. Young Harry was a big one too – had been from birth. His size nearly killed his mother when he arrived, they said, and he was going to be even bigger than his father. The son admired his father and was proud of the fact it took at least three strong men to take him down. The boy took his father's bully lessons to heart and terrorized the smaller boys in the village. In turn, he regularly got a cuffing from their bigger brothers and even from their parents.

After his father died, the boy was no longer Young Harry. He became, in his mind, Harry, The Man of the House. Although relatives and neighbors took pity on Agnes and her family and helped care for them, Harry felt obliged to hustle for pennies, doing whatever work a child his age could find. Because of his size and strength, he could do the work of a ten year old and toiled hard on neighboring farms whenever he could get out of school.

At school, Harry was an impossible child for the teachers to handle. He was a troublemaker and was insolent even to the headmaster. He was caned often and sent home with warning after warning. By the time he was eleven, he was out of school more than he was in and that's when he turned to working full time on the farm of a sympathetic neighbor.

At fifteen he left home and joined the army, easily passing for eighteen. He very quickly became a happy young man and a good soldier. He sent almost his entire pay home to his mother, proud that he had fully replaced his father as the head of the household.

In his army training, his bullying and bravado turned into leadership and bravery. Young as he was, he was able to goad his comrades to take chances and to throw themselves into their training with gusto. He was always the first to try new and dangerous exercises and he did so with a laugh and a holler. The live ammunition the instructors sometimes used in training just made him more exuberant.

Live ammunition became serious business in 1914 when nineteen-year-old Sergeant Harry Cameron and his infantry regiment sailed for France at the outbreak of the First World War. They lived the horrors of trench mud and rats and the terror of bayonet charges and rolling artillery barrages. Harry was decorated three times for bravery under fire and by 1917, when he went home on leave, he was the Regimental Sergeant Major.

His old headmaster was at the train to meet the hero, along with most of the village. His mother and sisters gave him monstrous hugs and then just gazed at him in awe, so handsome he was in his uniform and ribbons, so old he was in his face. He was a stranger to them and they were almost unknown to him. He couldn't get used to the sight of his own pastoral Scottish village after what he had seen in France where buildings were demolished and forests were burnt to ashes, where people hunted for food on roadsides, and children called out vainly for their mothers. He struggled to find his bearings.

Among the people at the station was a young girl of eighteen who, he later learned, had been helping his mother at the market stall where they sold vegetables and sausages. Harry was attracted first by the girl's shyness - the only one there who wasn't clamoring after him – and then by her red hair and sweet face and slight figure. He walked straight through the crowd to her side, politely introduced himself and asked her name.

He was more than a foot taller than she was but she dropped her eyes and answered, "I'm Helen MacLeod, Sergeant Cameron."

"It is Harry, lass. And where d'ye come from, Helen MacLeod? Yu're nae from this poor village."

"From over Dunvegan, Sergeant Cameron. My folks died and I'm living here with my aunt."

"Well, Helen MacLeod, would you please walk with me while you tell me what has been going on here since I left. And please, Lassie, call me Harry."

When Harry returned to France he carried a lock of Helen MacLeod's hair in his pocket and she carried his baby in her womb. Three weeks later he was killed in action.

Chapter Thirteen

James Cameron

"There's no more James. That's the last of it. The whole world is starvin' and now so are we." Helen MacLeod slumped forward onto the table, her forehead against the rough oak planking, her thin bony arms around her head, her shoulders heaving with her sobbing.

"What'll we do then, Mom?" Her son sat wide-eyed, alarmed at his mother's apparent surrender. He had never seen her like this, never heard her cry. They had been down to their last few pennies before but always she had held her head high. Now, he thought, things must be very bad.

He put his hand on her shoulder to reassure her. In his firmest twelve year old voice he said, "Mom, I can get a job. I'll earn some money. We'll be fine. You'll see." He listened to himself speaking and realized he had suddenly grown up.

She raised her head and forced a weak smile through her tears. "You can't do that, James. Your school. And who will hire you? No one can get a job these days. There's not even odd jobs for your stepdad, and your Grandma's market stall hardly pays pennies, so how can anyone pay for a twelve year old? It's no use James." She pulled him to her and again broke into loud sobs.

Early the next morning, before anyone was awake, James left the house and walked to the district's biggest farm two miles from the village. No one was around. He saw some firewood in a large heap by the woodshed where someone had sawn and chopped it. He set to work and piled it all neatly inside the shed. Then he walked over to the stable and began shoveling out the horse stalls. As he was finishing the last stall, an angry voice shouted, "What's goin' on here? You, boy. Who the hell are ye? Get outa my stable!"

The boy straightened up to his tallest height and said firmly, in his new grown up voice, "I'm James Harry Cameron, Sir. I want to work."

The man squinted at him with one eye. "Cameron are ye? The Sergeant Major's son?"

The boy looked him straight in the eye. "Yes sir."

"Well I see yu're already workin'. I suppose yu're wantin' t'be paid?"

"I can work hard, Sir. I'm strong like my father. And you can pay me whatever you want to, Sir."

It was after dark when James got home that night. As he came in the door, his mother grabbed him and hugged the breath out of him. "Where on earth have you been, my wee lad?" She held him away from her to get a good look at him. "I've been worried sick, James. You're alright, are ye?"

James held out his fist and, grinning, opened it to reveal a sixpence coin.

He began working full time at the farm and never set foot inside the schoolroom again.

It wasn't that he didn't like school. Unlike his father before him, he was a good student, top of his class in fact, and his teacher loved him for his good manners and his willingness to learn. He wasn't as big as his father had been at the same age, but he was still taller than most of his classmates and a very good athlete. His classmates liked him and looked up to him as the best footballer, for his age, in the district. As he thought about his life though, only one thing bothered him: he would never become the military hero his sergeant major father was, because, people said, after World War I, wars were a thing of the past.

His mother often spoke to him about his father, stroking and kissing the only picture of him that existed, a formal portrait in uniform which Harry Cameron – Young Harry - had had taken on his last leave. She kept his medals in a tin biscuit box, carefully wrapped with a soft cloth, and on each anniversary of the Sergeant Major's birthday she would open them up with gentle hands and show them to James.

She had not been a bit ashamed that she had become pregnant by the Sergeant without being married. Furthermore, when James was born she insisted he carry the Cameron surname, proud she was that she was the mother of the hero's child.

Helen did get married in 1920, mainly out of pity for a returned soldier who had spent more than a year in hospital with shell shock and head wounds. The doctors had finally turned him out when his memory loss got no better. He was just twenty years of age, the same as Helen, but his hair had turned pure white. He was from a nearby village, a mild uncommunicative man. When addressed he just smiled rather blankly, his way of handling his confusion, a kind of excuse. However, he was kind and willing, and with Helen's help he found work doing odd jobs at the general store. They soon had three children even while Helen continued at the market. Young as he was, James pitched in as a household helper and babysitter.

Helen needn't have worried about James dropping out of school. Within days of starting to work, he began spending his evenings pouring over the schoolbooks which he had persuaded his headmaster to lend him. He collared some of his friends who were still in school to get their daily assignments, and when he checked his progress against theirs, he found he was more than able to keep up. Everyone, even his mother, was amazed at his determination to educate himself. "Father left school before twelve, Mom, and he made his mark, didn'e? So, don't fret. I'll do the same."

When he was fifteen, James spoke with the manager of the village bank about a part-time apprenticeship as an accountant. "I'm very good with figures, Sir, and ye needn't pay me a penny. I can get up early enough to finish my work at the farm by three o'clock in the afternoon and be here by three-thirty every day. On Sunday morning I just work two hours at the farm and then my Mom lets me study after Kirk." When he was seventeen, James left his farm job and was working full time at the bank, studying in the evening and playing football on Saturday afternoon, all the while providing support for his family.

On rare occasions, when he had a spare hour, he liked to walk across the highlands by himself, soaking up the smell of the peat fires and the heather, and drenching himself in the feel of the land. Something happened to him on these walks. The silence, the space, the nature – what was the magic? He spoke of it to no one; only, "It takes me somewhere, Mom."

By nineteen, James was the senior clerk in one of the bank's larger branches a half-hour bicycle ride from his home. He was a quick learner, his number skills were as good as any clerk they had ever had, and he had a wonderful way with people. His superiors knew they had a winner on their hands. He was on his way up the ladder.

Then came the bombs of September 1939.

Chapter Fourteen

The Commencement Address

"Today, in this final commencement of the twentieth century, we are honoring seven men and women who, during this past century, have given their lives to the betterment of humankind. How they have lived and worked is a testament to the indomitable human spirit. Their sense of a higher mission, their acts of courage, and their incredible accomplishments are an inspiration to all of us as we seek to fulfill our own opportunities for service in the twenty-first century. This university marks their contributions by conferring upon them our honorary degrees. They honor us by their presence.

"The seven come from seven different countries. They have taken their actions into seven different areas of our lives. But we honor them together because, for all seven, their field of action is the world and their common goal is peace.

"One of the seven is an environmentalist whose words and deeds over a period of nearly fifty years have asked us to take heed of our natural world and asked us to be at peace with our planet. Another is a medical doctor, born in this state and an alumnus of this university, who, since her graduation from medical school fifty years ago, has worked in rural villages in Asia and Africa, bringing peace to the sick. Next we have a photo journalist who has been traveling from war to war to war, wielding his weapon of peace - his compassionate eye - which he has focused on the suffering of civilians and soldiers alike. Peace of the soul, and thus of the world, is the work of another of our honorees, a nuclear physicist who has been showing us the reality of the abstract human spirit in her language of particle physics. Another is a tireless pilgrim for peace who, working behind the scenes and against long odds, has successfully negotiated agreements on missiles and land mines and hostages and borders and ethnic integration. And we honor a woman who, this month, will mark fifty-five years of service in organizations which aid refugees. And she continues her work to bring peace to the traumatized lives of the displaced. The seventh, and our commencement speaker today, is an international banking authority who, at an age when most people are well and truly retired, is still traveling as an advisor to developing countries in his long quest for stable and ethical economies as a foundation for peace."

The President looked down to the rows of black-robed students in the front half of the hall, their parents and friends arrayed behind them and in the balconies above. This was the day for graduate students to parade across the platform and receive their Masters and Ph.D. degrees. The students looked up attentively as the President leaned forward on the lectern, lowered her voice, slowed her cadence, and spoke especially to them. "As you hear about the contributions of each of these giants among us, let us consider how their lives paint the picture of this expiring century, the picture of us - humanity – as we have evolved in these last hundred years, and especially in these last fifty years, the time when our honorees have been most active in their work for peace." The President paused before concluding, "And let us consider how we - all of us – might carry forward their mission of peace, each of us in our own way."

The President acknowledged the applause, then stepped away to relinquish her place to the Dean of the Faculty of Science. In the colorful doctoral robes of his own alma mater, the Dean swirled to the lectern, scanned the audience to take in the whole hall, then intoned deeply, "Herr Doctor Wolfgang Helmut Schaeffer. Would you please come forward?"

As the audience applauded warmly, two faculty members helped the well-dressed, elderly Austrian environmentalist stand up, and then supported him as he shuffled slowly to the center of the platform. Another brought a chair and seated him facing the audience. The Dean began to read the citation which would lead to the Honorary Doctor of Science degree.

The international banker's twenty-year-old grandson, sitting in the center of the front row of the balcony, surveyed the scene before him. This was Ian Cameron's first trip to America and he was absorbing every moment. His eyes focused on his grandfather, James Harry Cameron, sitting in the front row beside the other honorees. The man already had several honorary degrees and still the grandson's pride welled up and constricted his chest. His stomach tightened for a moment as he thought about his grandmother who had died a year earlier. How he wished she could have been here beside him to share in the pride.

He softened his focus and gazed across the platform which held about a hundred faculty members wearing academic robes of purple and crimson and gold and blue, and some colors he couldn't put a name on. Behind the faculty sat the orchestra, about thirty strong, with a lot of brass shining in the bright lights. The state Governor sat to the side of the faculty with the Chair of the Board of Trustees, both in black gowns with hoods in the colors of the university. The flags of the dozens of countries from which the graduating students came, countries on six continents, decorated the walls of the hall – this midwestern university was proud of its strong commitment to international understanding. The American flag was in the center at the back of the platform, flanked by the State flag and the University insignia and the flags of the seven nations which were home to the honorary degree recipients. The motto of the university was inscribed on the arch above the flags: Strength in Diversity; Harmony in Action. The grandson thought about whether that motto would have suited his Cambridge college.

At the end of the citation the Dean presented the Austrian to the President, then stood behind the environmentalist and placed a hood over his shoulders. The old man grasped the hand of the President, and then the hand of the Dean. In the warmth of the audience applause, they helped him back to his place. Then in succession, the Deans of other faculties called forth the honorary recipients, read their citations, conferred the degrees, and retired. The citations were lengthy, detailing not only their achievements but also much about their personal backgrounds. The message was clear – this was about lives richly lived, not just life outcomes. And it was about the fabric of the twentieth century.

The Dean of the School of Management was the last to take the lectern. "Sir James Harry Cameron." He announced. "Would you please come forward, sir?"

The Sergeant Major's son rose easily from his chair and smiled to the applauding audience. He looked up at the balcony, found his grandson, and gave him an exaggerated wink before walking across the platform to stand before the Dean. His gait was steady and his movement still fluid despite his eighty-one years. His broad shoulders were rounded slightly and his head bent forward a few degrees, but his demeanor was bright and he was still an impressive figure of strength and determination.

"When James Harry Cameron was twelve years old," the Dean began, "the Great Depression of the 1930s, which infected the world, overwhelmed his Scottish family. To help support them, James Cameron left school and went to work on a farm. That was the end of his classroom education. This afternoon we will confer on him his eighth honorary doctorate."

The Dean paused and dipped his head to look out over his reading glasses at the graduating class. "I would like our new graduates to take note," he said. A ripple of laughter showed the audience's appreciation.

"When he was fifteen," continued the Dean, "he started working four hours a day at the bank in his Scottish village - without pay - so he could learn about business. This was after he had finished some eight or nine hours of work at the farm."

The Dean paused again, looked over his glasses, and slowly intoned, "I would like our MBA graduates to take note." There was more wry laughter and scattered applause from the audience.

"Even though he left the classroom, he never left learning – something I think all of us might note. By studying at night and on weekends he more than kept pace with his former classmates. At seventeen, the bank hired him full time – for pay – and he progressed rapidly until the Second World War arrived on Britain's shoulders in 1939.

"He immediately joined the Royal Air Force and flew Spitfires in the Battle of Britain. Sir James speaks little about those years but the record shows he was awarded the Distinguished Flying Cross three times and ended the war as a Wing Commander. He will only say about those times that, if you were lucky enough to survive, you were promoted."

The grandson, his elbows on the balcony rail, chin resting on his fists, listened hard to the story of his grandfather. He had heard pieces of it here and there over the years but never a coherent narrative like this.

"He returned to the bank's London offices after the war and worked his way rapidly up the management ranks in the bank's international division with postings in Hong Kong, Johannesburg, Bombay, Sao Paulo and New York. Government officials in these countries, and in the adjoining countries falling within his regional responsibility, began to call him Britain's Finance Ambassador because of the concern he showed for the economic welfare of their countries and their people.

"His success in these postings, according to his colleagues, was because he managed the bank with great sensitivity to the cultures in which he worked. According to Sir James, his success was because of the influence of his late wife, Dorothy. She constantly reminded him, he says, that his job was first about people, and only second about money. Nevertheless, he had a brilliant financial mind which took him back to London in 1961 to take charge of the bank's rapidly growing international operations.

"Just three years later he became Managing Director of the bank and in 1970, at age fifty-two, he became Chairman, the youngest ever to hold that office in his company. His appointment coincided with the beginning of the decade of turbulence which hit all of the world's economies and he quickly put measures in place which would shepherd the bank through to safe ground.

"As he did so, senior politicians in the United Kingdom called on him regularly for advice on banking regulations and economic policy. For his banking achievements, and for his services to the government, he was knighted by the Queen.

"Senior politicians in other countries, whom he had known from his expatriate days, also called on him for assistance. He became an advisor to Presidents and Prime Ministers and Tribal Chiefs.

Their challenges were so great and his compassion for their people was so deep, he left the Chairmanship after just six years, took early retirement from the bank, and devoted his life to helping those countries which seemed to need him most.

"For the past twenty-five years, then, he has been working tirelessly and without remuneration to strengthen the governing structures and the institutions of nations in the developing world. He has helped several countries to stabilize their economies and has been forceful in demanding the ethical handling of the people's money. He has helped these nations to feed, educate and bring health care to their people, and thus has helped to bring peace to these often troubled lands.

"Sir Harry is today the world's foremost authority on the financial infrastructures of developing countries. Through his skill and dedication, he has brought successful resolution to seemingly impossible problems, and in doing so has made literally millions of lives more livable. He has also given this university great service as a wise counselor and supporter of our international programs. However, he is much more than a banker, much more than an international authority, much more than a war hero, much more than anything we have described. He is above all, in his person and in his profession, a man of peace.

"Mr. President, I commend to you, for the degree of Doctor of Laws, Honoris Causa, Sir James Harry Cameron."

To sustained applause, the President shook the banker's hand warmly and the Dean placed the hood over Sir James' shoulders.

Then the Dean introduced Sir James as the Commencement Speaker.

Sir James opened his address with appropriate formality: "Governor, Mister Chairman, Madam

President, Dean Davidovic, distinguished members of the faculty, graduating students, ladies and gentlemen."

Ian listened to his grandfather speak his appreciation for the work of all of the other honorary degree recipients, and give his thanks to the university for his award. As he listened, Ian's mind hovered between speculation about his own future life and appreciation for the incredible life his grandfather had lived. Ian saw that as a twenty-year-old he was standing, as it were, between two centuries, and between two lives. Here were two stories - one coming to an end, the other just beginning.

Somewhere in the middle of the two stories was Ian's father, Harry MacLeod Cameron, named after Sir James' parents, the Sergeant Major and Helen MacLeod. Although Ian and his father, known as Mac, saw one another infrequently, there was a strong bond of love between them. Still, Ian wished his father were more like Sir James - more outgoing, more adventuresome. Mac was hardly the bearer of the Cameron family tradition and, in fact, Ian called his father a bookworm. Mac had taken part in sports at school and continued to hike and cycle regularly, but he seemed to take sports as a pleasurable way to be physically fit rather than as a field of competition. Mac's sister, Ian's Aunt Patricia, was much more a Cameron, much more athletically inclined than Mac, and certainly more sociable. *Had the success genes skipped his father,* Ian wondered? But then, he thought, *maybe success wasn't a matter of genes. And maybe it wasn't a matter of winning trophies.*

In his own world, Ian was considered a great success – rugby captain, stroke on the college eight, leading cricket batsman, as well as an outstanding scholar, friend to all, and man about town. The town was Cambridge and Emmanuel College was the center of the world where he excelled. That was his world now. What about the future? As he listened to his grandfather speaking, Ian wondered, *What will I become in the great real world outside? Would I match the success of my grandfather's life? Could I?*

"This afternoon," Sir James said, "I would like to address my remarks especially to those of you who are about to leave behind these classrooms and laboratories and embark on a new phase of your journey. In the citations today we have heard something about the life of the century past. Now you are about to take on your shoulders the life of the century before us, and I wonder how your newly graduated eyes will view what lies ahead.

"For my part, I see a century where humanity will emerge from its shell and become the community we dream it could be."

He spoke without notes and without self-consciousness, as though he was chatting in his living room with friends. His baritone voice was rich and warm, enveloping everyone in the hall. Although he hadn't lived in Scotland for more than sixty years, his brogue still colored his speech, and his American audience loved it.

"We do have a shared dream, do we not? Your university has today given voice to that shared dream in citing the theme of peace in the work of the seven of us whom you have honored. We all dream, do we not, of peace among nations, peace among people of different races, colors, religions and ethnicity, peace in our communities and our families; peace in our hearts. Our dream of peace - is that not the ultimate dream for humanity?

"Why, our very essence," he almost whispered, "cries out for peace." He leaned forward and asked quietly but firmly, "Are we going to close our minds to that cry?"

Almost magically, the audience, as one, fell silent. The speaker's words, his voice, his very way of being, touched every heart, finding some fundamental common resonance within.

"We can't ignore it. The cry will not let us. Our deepest impulse will not let us.

"Our only way forward is to respond to that impulse. It is our only option."

The atmosphere his grandfather had created in the hall stunned Ian. He recognized there was something more than his words that had captured the audience and lifted their attention to a higher plane. Afterward, his grandfather would say something had captured him too, and he had heard himself speaking with some inner voice.

"It is our only option because, sooner or later, our deepest impulse wins. We cannot hold back the incoming tide.

"This deepest impulse, I believe, is the underlying bond which links us to our fellow humans – the bond that says we are one. We all know it at some level, do we not? We speak easily of 'the human family'. We all feel it, consciously or unconsciously, and it urges us from within, unremittingly, to express outwardly our underlying unity.

"History is marked by responses to that urge. After the French Revolution, that country adopted the motto: 'liberty, fraternity, equality'; that is humanity's deepest impulse speaking. President Lincoln expressed the impulse when he spoke of, 'a nation conceived in liberty and dedicated to the proposition that all men are created equal'. And look at the words above this platform – your university motto: 'Strength in Diversity; Harmony in Action.' That too speaks the impulse.

"So, how shall we now give greater form to the impulse? How shall we turn our dream into reality? Or, more correctly, how shall we turn our reality – for this impulse *is* reality, I believe - how shall we turn our reality into action?" He smiled at the audience, inviting them into his question. "How shall we bring into the light, and into our everyday lives, the awareness of the fact of the oneness of humanity so, through Harmony in Action, we will know peace on earth? How shall we do that?"

Sir James leaned back from the podium for a moment, leaving the question to do his talking. There was a silent space where small thoughts gathered up and merged with a larger idea, the proposition implicit in Sir James's question, the proposition that our destiny – peace - was in our hands. It was up to us. Too idealistic? Sir James read their doubts.

"Perhaps you think my question rests on a doubtful assumption," he smiled. "Perhaps you think we can't plot the course of a century to come, that we must sit back and await that power we call 'the universe' to unfold and tell us what to do. Well, I happen to think 'the universe' is waiting for us – waiting for us to decide whether our dream is worth the effort. It is waiting for us, I believe, to decide just how high we want to climb, this next century, up the ladder of our evolution.

"Are we prepared to decide? Are we prepared to act? Or are we content just to stroll passively into whatever the future casts our way? Hmm?"

Again, he paused for a moment, allowing the audience to engage with him, allowing them to think about where his questions were leading them.

"Shall we take a chance? Shall we turn our passive stroll into a march forward? Shall we decide that we are going ahead with all speed, that we are going to align ourselves with that inner impulse, with our inevitable human destiny, and turn these next hundred years into The Century of Peace on Earth?

"Our ancestors are looking down on us and waiting." He spoke slowly now, pausing between sentences. "Our children are looking up to us and waiting. All the world is waiting for peace to happen." He lengthened the pause. "In the words of Captain

Picard of the Starship Enterprise, let us 'make it so'. Let us make peace happen." He paused again, and surveyed all sections of the hall. He seemed to look directly into each person's eyes. The audience waited expectantly.

"I mean right now - right here. Let us make peace happen." He smiled, almost mischievously. "Are you ready?"

Seeing the puzzled looks, he smiled again and said, "Please humor me for a moment. Let this old man have his way. Allow me my dream." The audience murmured and smiled their agreement. By now he was their good friend.

"My dream, of course, is our dream - the dream of humanity." His words came from deep within his heart and all the hearts in the hall resonated together, all on the same wave length, all speaking as one.

"Please join with me to see if we can make peace happen - right here, right now. I would like everyone to relax, close your eyes, and take five minutes to imagine, in silence, your own picture of peace on earth. See, and feel, and for these five minutes, *live*, the peace of all-encompassing love. See, feel, *live* the peace of all-encompassing beauty - the peace of all-encompassingness."

Ian described later to his sister, Lisa, what had happened during that five minutes. "Quiet reigned. Absolute quiet. The hall, though, was alive. Really. It was electric. The hall seemed to vibrate as though we were in some great microwave oven. I swear it would have lit up the night."

To mark the end of the five minutes, Sir James said, quietly, "Thank you." The silence persisted. Then one man at the back of the balcony slowly clapped his hands together, then a few around him joined in, and then more, and more, until the hall was brimming with joyful applause and appreciation.

"Please, ladies and gentlemen," Sir James continued when the applause had subsided. "Please hold that vision of peace. Please make it your touchstone, your picture of where we are going and what we are going to create. And especially to our graduates, may your vision of peace on earth guide your every step into the twenty-first century."

Ian rose to his full Cameron height and joined with the rest of the audience in the long applause.

Chapter Fifteen

Ian Cameron

"Has Ian Cameron left college, Higgs?"

"He left a half hour ago, sir."

"He didn't even say goodbye."

"No Mr. Webster, he didn't say good-bye to anyone." The hall porter tilted his head and shrugged. "All he said was, 'I'll send for the rest of my things,' and then he just ran to the train station with his laptop and one bag."

"Isn't that the skids? It's not like Ian to leave college without saying goodbye."

When the call came from the Ministry, Ian had thrown some clothes into a suitcase and made a dash for the train in order to get to the office in London before it closed. It was the job he had been hoping for but someone else had been selected. Now, at the last minute, that someone had backed out and they needed a replacement – immediately. If Ian could get the paperwork done today and be on a flight tomorrow morning, he had the job.

"He did mention one other thing," the hall porter added.

"What was that?"

"Africa," said the hall porter. "He said he was going to work in Africa."

"Africa? And he's leaving tomorrow? Before graduation? He can't do that."

"I guess he can, Mr. Webster."

Ian was relieved to find an empty compartment on the train. It gave him space to think about this sudden turn of events, and a couple of hours to collect himself. This might be the last time he would take this train, he realized, the last time to see this familiar landscape between Cambridge and London. He had taken this trip for four years – how many times? Probably a dozen return trips a year. And now it was over. Could he accept that? The end had come too suddenly.

Four years. He remembered arriving in August four years earlier. It was a wet and dreary day. And cold. How could it be so cold in August? He and Simon Webster had checked into the Porter's Lodge at the same time and they had been best friends ever since. Simon didn't own a cell phone - didn't believe in them - or Ian would have called him to say goodbye. He reinforced a mental note to try to call Simon tonight in his quarters.

Simon, and many other friends, had been his family for four years. Cambridge had become his home. He loved Cambridge – the architecture of the colleges, the gardens, the museums. And he loved the evenings at the pub by the lock, and punting on the Backs with his girlfriend of the year, and going to the theatre, and listening to the King's College choir at Christmas, and rowing, and playing cricket and rugby. He was the finest batsman the College had produced in years, according to the old-timers who watched the matches. His eight had been second only to the all-Cambridge crew that beat Oxford. His rugby team had won its league.

But mostly he loved the intellectual challenge of the lectures, the give and take with his tutors and the endless debates with his fellow students in the Common Room. He read philosophy but considered himself well educated in history and sociology as well. For all his breadth of interests and activities, he earned first class honors - in fact, he ranked at the top of his college's academic lists in two of the four years.

And so it was ended.

Royston Station passed and he left thoughts of Cambridge behind and turned to what lay ahead of him. He took a deep breath and shook his head to clear his mind. He could hardly believe it. Africa. He was going to Africa. For three years. It was the continent of his dreams – dreams conjured out of the entrancing stories his grandfather had told him. Sir James had been on safari many times during his bank posting in Africa and on later advisory trips. He told of stalking lions and rhinoceros and elephants with only a Hasselblad as a weapon. But mostly he told of the beauty of the land and the people. Especially the people. He was fascinated with their ingenuity in making a livelihood in primitive circumstances, and he shared with his grandchildren his worries about what would become of these people as the modern world infiltrated their lives – or perhaps overran them.

Now I will be part of that infiltration, he thought. *Part of their problem.* A pang of doubt caught him in the gut. *Why am I taking this job*, he asked himself. *Is it an ego trip? Look at me, everyone. I am going to Africa to do good. Or am I trying to match my grandfather's achievements? Or is it just a tourist safari? All of these reasons?* He shifted uncomfortably and slouched, legs straight, feet under the opposite seat. It had seemed like such a good idea, and now, on the verge of leaving, he was questioning his motive. *Is it* really *a good idea? What is this job really about? What am I really about?*

He felt the rhythm of the train soothe his body. It brought some comfort and steadied his mind. He sat up straight, then, and followed the meditation process his father, Mac, had taught him. It relaxed his worries and allowed his thoughts to form slowly. After a few moments, a deeper realization started to emerge and his mind quietly surrounded it, formulated it, owned it. "It's okay," he heard himself say aloud. "It's okay. This is not about you. It is about some people who need help. Just listen to the people and you will know what to do."

The afternoon sun filled the desert sky and beat down on the tarmac, encouraging a hasty walk from the plane to the air-conditioned terminal. After passing painfully slowly through customs and immigration, Ian and his three companions gathered their luggage around them, eyes searching for whoever was supposed to meet them. They were going in pairs to two villages and their instructions said they would be met and driven by a government official from the district where the villages were located. They pushed their luggage into a heap on the floor, sat down, and waited. When night fell, they sprawled on the floor to sleep.

"Good morning, my friends," boomed the deep voice. "Good morning, and welcome."

Ian lifted his head off his duffel bag and squinted up at the voice. A big-toothed grin dominated the face behind the voice.

"I hope you slept well," boomed the happy voice. "We have a long drive today."

The four stiffly picked themselves up off the floor and shook hands with their greeter. He said nothing about being a day late and neither did they. He took the wheel of an old pickup truck beside two women and a small child, and the newcomers piled into the back with their luggage and four other passengers.

The morning parade had become a daily ritual. The children surrounded Ian, jumping and giggling and vying to hold his hand for the walk to the new well, singing a lilting melody about chasing the demons out from under their beds. The well was a mile from the village and now the elders had approved a pipeline to bring the water to the edge of the compound. Ian and his partner had led the well and pipeline project from behind the authority of the elders and had incorporated it into their school teaching. The children planned how the work should be done and how the water should be used and did calculations and wrote stories about it as part of their lessons. They also did as much of the physical work on the project as they were able. In the classroom, they were already starting on their next project – a cart path to the next village so they could exchange more farm produce than they could carry in baskets.

During his third year in the village, Ian received a brief e-mail message from Simon that his grandfather, Sir James, was ill and was asking for him. Ian wondered why his father hadn't contacted him. Ian's only sister, Lisa, who lived in America, might not know either, for she certainly would have called him if she did. Maybe his father didn't know – that was possible. There seemed to be a rift between his father and grandfather which stemmed, Ian believed, from Mac's inability to meet the expectations of his fighter pilot-banking executive-knighted statesman-father. Ian first suspected the rift as a young boy when Sir James had attributed Ian's athletic ability to his being a "real Cameron, unlike your father."

Like Ian's grandfather, both Ian and his father had the Cameron physique and the reddish blond hair of Helen MacLeod, but Ian's father was an introverted intellectual, not an extroverted adventurer. So withdrawn was he that he seldom left his home except to go to work or to go cycling or hiking. At Cambridge he was a student of history and philosophy, and by the time he graduated he had mastered five languages. He wrote poetry as a sideline and became an expert on Shakespearean theatre. His high intelligence was evident. None of that seemed to impress his father. When Sir James named his son 'Harry MacLeod Cameron' he had expected the boy to be just like his namesake, the Sergeant Major. In order to distance himself from the expectation, people said, the boy began calling himself "MacLeod," which became "Mac."

As soon as Ian got Simon's message, he phoned his sister Lisa in New York. Lisa said she knew nothing of their grandfather's illness. Ian then phoned his father. No answer. Then he called his father's sister, Aunt Patricia, in Australia. She said she had spoken to Sir James only a week earlier and he was making plans for a trip to Singapore and was going to detour to Perth to see her and her family. She doubted if Ian's father would know anything since, as far as she knew, the father and grandfather had not spoken to one another for more than two years. Ian winced at her words. Why did it have to be that way?

Ian folded his phone into his shirt pocket and thought about options. His grandfather had no family around him. Ian didn't know his grandfather's current housekeeper. His office? Since he traveled so much he worked in an office at home when he was in London, and his secretary worked from her home. *Surely, she would know. But then, why hadn't she called him?* He phoned the secretary and from her answering service he learned she would be back in two weeks. *Thank God for Simon Webster. Good old Simon.* He dialed Simon's apartment in London, praising the technology gods and satellites. He wondered if Simon had a mobile cell phone yet.

After speaking to Simon, Ian left immediately for London but he was too late. The doctor said it was a massive heart attack. There was a service in the cathedral attended by the nobility of society, business, and government. Ian's father was there, of course, but remained in the background as much as he possibly could under the circumstances. Mac was so inconspicuous, in fact, that some of the guests were more than a little surprised when he was introduced to them as the son of the deceased. Mac's sister Patricia could not make the trip from Australia because of a serious illness in her immediate family. Lisa had flown in from New York and graciously put people at their ease. Ian acted as the family head.

After the service and reception, their father took Ian and Lisa to dinner where he told them the truth about his relationship with their grandfather. "There was no rift between us. On the contrary - over these past ten years, we were able to establish a deep rapport with one another that did not require any personal contact. Do you understand? We met regularly - telepathically."

Ian and Lisa glanced at each other - did the other know about this?

"Perhaps it is time you knew something about my work. But let me be clear. I do not want you to speak about this to anyone. I want no publicity." The two nodded their agreement. Their father continued, "I have duties on this earth as part of an esoteric action which is preparing the way for an upswing in our planet's evolutionary impulse. I give these duties my intense and focused attention for periods of several hours every day. You know I make frequent hiking trips to Wales, to the Highlands, to the Norwegian mountains, and to the Alps, and on most weekends I go hiking somewhere in the countryside. I do that because, to be effective, I have to work as much as I can away from the noise of humanity. I can't tell you more than that, but it may give you a hint as to why my life has seemed reclusive."

On his way back to Africa on the British Airways 747, Ian pondered his father's life. When he was a young boy, family acquaintances had told Ian that Mac seemed to avoid, as much as he could, doing anything his distinguished father had done. People thought he had tried to get Sir James' approval by excelling in his own way – applying his broad intelligence to worldly affairs. It didn't work. His teachers attributed his limited socializing to the succession of countries and schools and nannies which came with his father's bank postings. Ian now realized these perceptions were ill-founded. The reality was something totally different.

Mac's parents had lived the busy social life of the expatriate business executive in the politically sensitive financial sector and had very little time for their two children. Mac seemed to cope by keeping to himself and working hard to get good grades – and at this he was an undoubted success. In the same environment, however, his sister Patricia had become very adept socially. But then she had withdrawn from the Cameron spotlight too, in a way, by going to Australia where she met and married her husband.

Mac's apparent shyness persisted at Cambridge and afterward. He went to work for the foreign office where he was considered a brilliant linguist, a creative political analyst, and a genius as a geopolitical visionary. His most competent and intelligent co-worker, a pretty young economist, admired his intelligence and found his shyness attractive. This was enough to win the attention of the very young and socially inexperienced genius. She was also attracted, it turned out, by his family's social standing and Sir James' money – it would go well with her own family's long history of near-royalty.

Mac and Cecelia were married in an elaborate formal ceremony in the garden of her parents' home in Sussex. Within four years Ian and Lisa were born, within six years Cecelia's social ambitions and Mac's retiring manner were an evident mismatch and she found other company, and within ten years they were divorced. The children stayed with their father who employed a grandmotherly nanny to care for them and keep house. Within a year their mother remarried and soon became a prominent and busy London socialite. They saw her often for the first few years until she seemed to be too busy to spend much time with them, and then she moved to the south of France somewhere and disappeared from their lives altogether.

The two children grew very close to their father and to the nanny. Then the nanny died and a few years later Ian and Lisa left home to go to university. Their father had lived alone since then, his only company a mixed breed dog from the Humane Society.

Ian closed his eyes and relived the conversation with his father and Lisa. He felt relieved that his father's retiring manner was not a weakness after all and that the connection with Sir James was just the opposite of what it seemed. He could also, now, appreciate more his father's encouraging his two children to meditate and to read the Bhagavad Gita. He was still surprised and puzzled, though, by the part about his father's esoteric duties.

They were an odd family, he thought. Family - what was that? Simon and the crowd at the College had been his family for four years. Now the African people he worked with were his family, and the village was his home. Another hour's flying time, according to the schedule, plus another day's tortuous truck ride, and he would be at that home. He warmed at the prospect of being back in the village and seeing his current family again.

Ian shaded his eyes and watched the single engine Cessna circle over the village before letting down on the grassy plain beyond the cultivated land. The whole village, from old hobbling grandmothers to babes in arms, scrambled to see who was coming. Except for Ian and his co-worker, the villagers had not seen anyone from the outside for almost a year. Ian felt an unusual air of anticipation as the plane taxied toward the compound. It shut down well before anyone could get close to the spinning propeller. The door swung open and out stepped a dark haired, athletic-looking woman, dressed in khaki shirt and slacks. She ducked from under the wing and walked, smiling brightly, toward the gathered crowd. The pilot stayed with the plane.

"Hello," she called.

"Hello," came the answering chorus of children who swarmed around her. The adults stood silently.

She stopped short and scanned the crowd for the Chief. He stepped forward. Then she spotted Ian and his project partner at the back of the throng, grinning at her as they waited to see how she would manage her introduction. She turned again to the Chief and asked if she might speak to him in English. He nodded, and they began.

After the preliminaries with the Chief, Ian approached her, took her by the hand, and led her toward the huts without even asking her name. "I know you," he said. "Do you know me?"

"No. I don't think so." She laughed. "Is this how you always chat up the birds?"

"I don't know your name but I love you," he declared impulsively, "and I am going to marry you."

"Oh, really?" She was taken aback, astonished. Then amused. She smiled, about to counter with her own joke. He wasn't smiling. She looked into his eyes and became serious. "Well, maybe you are."

She was Eva Rivera, a French biochemist, researching the nutritional needs of rural Africans. She worked out of London for a UN agency that set specifications for commercial developers of food supplements, as part of a new millennium program to eliminate malnutrition everywhere in the world. In the past three weeks her pilot had taken her to twenty villages. All had welcomed her even though they knew very little about the UN. They had let her examine the pupils of their eyes, take blood samples and hair samples, and samples of the soil where they grew their crops. Her smile was her passport; her compassion was the key to their hearts.

Ian's assignment in Africa ended two months after Eva's visit and he returned immediately to London. Two weeks later Ian Cameron and Eva Rivera were married.

Chapter Sixteen

Ian and Eva Cameron

"We're going to have a baby, Maman. Ian and I are going to have a boy."

"Oh, Eva. C'est magnifique! I will be a grandmother - and I am not even fifty. Oh, wait until your father hears. But how do you know it will be a boy? Did you get tests already?"

"No, Maman. I just know."

"You just know. Yes, I suppose you do. Et bien, when will he arrive?

"Next August. Maybe on your birthday."

"Merci, ma petite. Un cadeau magnifique! What a wonderful birthday present."

"You know, Ian, when the baby arrives it will be chaos. Your life will change in ways you never imagined."

Ian's father could foresee how life might unfold for people. He thought in terms of themes – streams of events, all possible problems as well as opportunities. It was one of the reasons he was the most valued analyst in his department.

"I know, Dad. I've read the books. What I see is nothing but exciting. Imagine – a new person to care for and nourish and help to find a place in the world. Eva loves children and you know how much I do."

"Eva, you hardly know this bloke - and you married him?"

"Three months ago."

"And you are really married to him? Church and all?"

"Not only married to him, Janet. We're having a baby."

"A baby? Oh, brilliant. You've really done it, girl."

"Haven't I though? Oh Janet, I may be crazy but I'm thrilled."

"That's obvious. So, tell me. Who is this Prince Charming?"

"His name is Ian Cameron and he works at the Ministry of the Environment. At least that's where he will be working starting next week."

"And?"

"And he's got reddish blond hair and blue eyes and he's over six feet tall and he has this perpetual smile that makes you want to hug him."

"Just perfect, Eva. You married blue eyes and a smile. That's lovely. Eva my dear, you have really lost it. I wish you good luck with the stranger."

"Oh, he's not a stranger, Janet. I feel as though I have known him forever. When we met we just immediately – you know – as though we had been waiting for each other to arrive."

"Aiya, I see you are resonating even more finely to the frequency of that young Cameron couple."

"I think we will be together, Ohruu."

"Their love for one another is a clear invitation to an incarnating soul."

"Yes, Ohruu, I hear it. And their due date matches my astrological plans."

Chapter Seventeen

The First Appearance

Moscow old-timers said they had never seen a worse winter than this one. It was still only February, so winter was far from over. They had never seen worse food shortages since the new President took over five years earlier. Some said it was as bad as the worst years of the Second World War. The dark days of 2005 would be remembered in the nation's history books.

The heavy cloud cover threw a cloak of despair over the hearts of the thousands of people who were suffering the cold without enough food or heating fuel or shelter. The snow piled high in the streets. No vehicles moved. The wind blew relentlessly; the blizzard seemed without end.

In spite of the improvements made over the past five years in the appearance of the city, there remained an underworld of crime and poverty. Gangs of thugs and corrupt police still controlled the streets, organized crime permeated the commercial world, and white-collar mini-czars in the government still ransacked public coffers as they had always done in Russia. Civility seemed to be present only among groups of the poorest citizens trying to survive together in a spirit of community. They huddled, in unheated buildings, in back street shacks, in lean-tos under bridges and in parks, sharing whatever scraps of food they could scrounge and whatever warmth their makeshift shelters and small fires could provide. These people with no possessions were the city's last vestige of the ideal of brotherhood which had shown such promise in the country ninety years earlier before it was snuffed out by Party despots.

By the middle of February, people were in desperate straits. For one of the most desperate back alley groups, the end was near. Their small fire flickered out, and though they clung together in a bundle, their ragged coats were no match for the cold. One by one they stopped shivering as hypothermia set in. Then there was no sign of life – they had survived together and now they would die together.

Suddenly the clouds parted briefly and the sun flashed through the gray winter sky. A great beam of light shone down on the silent huddle. A body moved, then rose from the ground and stood up. Another stirred, as though slowly coming awake, and sat up, and then another, until all in the huddle had come to life. They looked up at the first to stand, a tall woman who appeared to be within an aura of white light. They were frightened at first, but then they were enveloped by a warmth unlike any they had ever known, a warmth that filled them with joy as well as with life.

The woman smiled and held out her hand to those around her, offering them assistance in rising from the pavement. Their lights joined with hers, creating a vibrant harmonic which radiated an immense and powerful love. She invited them to go with her, into the streets, where they would bring their love to others.

Chapter Eighteen

The Awakenings

"What's in this package Tiffany? United States Postal Service Special Delivery. It's addressed to you, Tiff. From newharmonygifts.com. It's not heavy. What's in it? Can I open it?"

"No, Travis, you cannot. It's your Christmas present."

"My Christmas present? In February? Well then, you are really getting ahead of the rush."

"Maybe I'll let you have it for your birthday."

"Thanks, Honey, but that's still a month away. Let me guess what it is."

"You'll never guess."

"It's a set of containers to organize all the junk on my workbench."

"Not even close, my dear. Please take it upstairs when you go up to change and put it under the bed. And promise not to peek."

"Okay, I promise. Can I shake it?"

"No. And hurry back down. Dinner's almost ready."

As Travis went upstairs, his sport jacket over one arm, the parcel under the other, he started to loosen his collar and tie while his mind searched through the list of possible gifts Tiffany might have ordered. He turned into their bedroom and stopped abruptly. In the full-length mirror on the opposite wall he saw an angelic presence. His eyes widened. He blinked, and the image was gone. It was only there for a second, but he knew there was work for him to do.

That evening, Travis and Tiffany decided to go ahead with plans to travel to the village where their Foster Parent Plan child lived. They would adopt the whole village and would enlist the support of their friends and family to ensure the health and education needs of the entire village would be met. They hoped the adoption idea would spread to other compassionate groups in their community and beyond.

It was a quarter after twelve and past the usual bedtime for Betty and Andrew. They had been to an evening performance at the opera house and they lived an hour out of Sydney. So when they climbed into bed and turned off the lights, they were ready for sleep. Then the whistle on the kettle started to blow. Betty sat up and flicked on the light.

"Andrew, the kettle. I didn't leave the stove on. You must have done after you made your tea."

"That was ages ago. It wasn't me, darlin'."

"Well, please – you go and fix it, will you? I've been up and down those stairs a dozen times today."

Andrew hauled himself out of bed, put on his dressing gown and slippers, and disappeared down the stairs.

"Betty. Come down here, Love. You'll hafta see this."

"See what?" she grumbled as she stomped down the stairs.

"It's bloody mysterious, it is."

"See what?" she questioned as she arrived in the kitchen.

"Look. The stove was not on. The kettle was on the counter, and the water is cold. How did this bloody thing blow its whistle?"

"It must have been something else. Something outside."

They went back to bed and were soon asleep. Betty drifted into a dream about being on a train with Andrew, heading west from Sydney. The train's whistle blew and Betty woke up. She sat up in bed and listened. Was it the kettle again? She heard nothing, so pulled the cover over her head, refusing to think about it, and immediately went back to sleep.

Within minutes the dream and the whistle repeated and she awoke again, disturbed and a little frightened. She shook Andrew awake and, before his eyes were open, she started telling him her dream.

"No way." he blurted, sitting bolt upright. She continued telling the dream. "No way." He laughed incredulously. "That was my dream too."

She stared at him in disbelief. "The same dream?"

"You and I were in some kind of observation car on the train," he said.

"That was my dream too."

"We were heading west from Sydney, and the train blew its whistle at a crossing called 'Next', and we kept coming to the same crossing, and the train kept blowing its whistle."

"Next? Next what?"

"I don't know. Just Next, as though it was a message telling us to watch out for what's coming next."

They turned together and held one another silently in a close embrace. In their silence, they knew their work had begun. Next morning, Andrew awoke with a complete action plan formulated in his mind. He contacted several key people in his world-wide network of journalists to establish a cooperative internet forum for the development of new ideas to achieve world peace. Betty initiated a similar international forum for new ideas to resolve issues of nutrition and healthy living for the millions of people displaced by war and natural disasters. Both knew that new solutions were possible to old problems because of the shift in world energy patterns.

In only a year, the little business Zeid and Nadir had started in a stall at the market had grown into a busy shop on one of Amman's main commercial streets. In spite of their success, the couple continued to work as hard as ever, driven by a compelling desire for financial independence. Their children helped out at the shop but not at the expense of their schooling, for education was to be their passport to the West. Zeid and Nadir were proud and loving parents and their children's future was the focus of their family life. Nadir often said of her children, "They're as bright as the sun, as beautiful as the moon, and as wise as the stars."

One evening, around the time of the February full moon, Zeid and Nadir were closing up their shop when a flash of light blinded their eyes. It was so seeringly white that Zeid thought it was an atomic bomb. They dropped to their knees in terror, clinging to one another, afraid they were never going to see their children again, afraid their end had come.

"We must have waited five minutes before we opened our eyes," Zeid related to the neighbors who had gathered to hear their story.

"It was an eternity." Nadir sighed, reliving the moment. "I wondered, were we still alive? Were we dreaming?" She shook her head, still bewildered, yet there was a serenity about her.

"And now," Zeid explained, "we are going back home to the West Bank. We are taking our children and we are going to work for peace among our people and with our neighbors. Our lives are changed and our future is waiting before us."

Nadir continued softly, "In the name of Allah, we are going to teach love."

The retired truck driver stirred the heap of sugar he had put in his coffee and smiled at the story related to him by the young man who sat opposite in the restaurant booth. The old trucker remembered when he was that age and had the same excitement about life. Only this twenty-five year old had actually engaged that youthful excitement in something worthwhile. For the past year, he had lived in the high arctic in the Canadian territory of Nunavut, helping people in small scattered communities to use computers for education and for linking with the rest of the world.

"You should go up there some time," the young man said. "It's amazingly beautiful."

The warmth in the young man's eyes touched the trucker. "So, Kyle, you hitched a ride on a cargo plane from up there – whad'ya call that place?"

"Iqaluit. It's the capital of Nunavut. It's on southern Baffin Island."

"Right. Iqaluit to Winnipeg. And now you're going to hitch-hike on the highway from Winnipeg to Montreal?"

"That's right."

"Man, it's February and this is the Canadian prairie. You'll freeze."

"I'll make it."

"What's in Montreal?"

"Montreal is home. At least it used to be, eh? My family is gone now. The arctic is my home today. I wish I could go back there right now and keep on working with the Inuit. They are a wonderful people, you know. But for now, Montreal is where I can get a job. In a year or two I'll have enough money to go back up north and continue with the work."

"You don't get paid for what you do?"

"I sometimes earn a little doing computer projects for a few companies and government offices, but I need money to buy equipment for my students. My real pay is the pleasure of living and working

112

there. They are a very generous people but there are lots of social problems in the communities. I try to help wherever I can."

"You want to live up there - permanently?"

"You bet I do."

"That's really something – all that cold and everything."

"I don't mind - there's a lot of warmth in the people. Besides, the arctic landscape is a place of great beauty."

"I see where your heart is, young man."

"Well, I'd better get going. Thanks very much for the coffee and sandwich. I hope we meet again some time." Kyle put on his ragged parka, picked up his well-traveled packsack, and shook the trucker's hand.

"Now, wait just a minute, Kyle," the trucker said. "Why don't you let me pay for a bed for you at that motel over there and then we'll see what tomorrow brings?"

"Really? Why, thank you again. I could sure use a good sleep before I hit the road."

Next morning, Kyle emerged from the shower, refreshed and ready to travel. Then he noticed his old parka was gone and a new one hung in its place. His old packsack was gone too, replaced by a new one full of new clothes. In the outer pocket of the packsack was a plane ticket to Iqaluit and a wallet with some twenty-five thousand dollars in cash.

The cold arctic front, which reached down from Siberia, made it a bright, crisp winter day in Tokyo. Kenkichi and Kyoko hurried along the Ginza to the fabric shop where they would buy some lengths of kimono silk. Businessmen were coming from Paris to visit Kenkichi's company and the silk would be gifts for their wives.

At the front of the fabric shop, Kyoko paused before entering. Something on the pavement had caught her eye. She stooped to pick it up. It was a large, brightly shining coin, unlike any she had seen before. It was white gold with silver markings but it had no inscription and no money value indicated. On one side was a raised five-pointed star, one point much longer than the others and reaching to a small circle on the edge of the coin. The other side was a single line, as though cutting the coin into two equal parts. As she examined it, the star started to shine even more brightly. Kyoko was mesmerized by it – as though it was meant for her.

"Come on, Kyoko," her husband urged.

Didn't Kenkichi see this on the sidewalk, she wondered as she put it into her pocket and hurried to catch up to him? Was it only for her? Kyoko felt the coin pressing into her hand as she held it in her pocket. It was for Kenkichi too. It was telling her something. Yes. She knew what it was.

The following weekend, after the visitors had left, Kyoko and Kenkichi decided they would establish a retreat center for business people to find the higher purpose in their work as leaders of thousands of employees. The couple would share their considerable intuitive skills to inspire their guests to act from their connection with the power of the Love Impulse.

"Joao. Wake up. We're ready to sail." Tomaz called again to his sleeping brother in the bunk below deck and again got no response. He turned to his fiancée and said, "Teresa, you and Isobelle can handle the anchor. Joao will be awake and up here as soon as we are under way."

The breeze was light, but as long as it held steady, it would be enough to get them home to the marina south of Rio de Janeiro before dark. Under the clear sky, the hours passed gently. The four friends lazed in the warm sun, communicating with few words, thinking few thoughts – a fitting conclusion to their ten-day sailing holiday. Tomorrow would be soon enough to write on the clean slates of their minds.

The breeze freshened a little and Tomaz asked Joao to give a half-turn to the mainsheet. That was when the lightning struck.

By the time they stepped onto land that evening, the four had decided how to respond to the flashes of insight that had changed their world. From their senior positions in the financial infrastructure of Brazil, they would use their intuition, their intelligence, and their well-developed persuasive arts to revolutionize the way the great wealth of their country was distributed among its people. It was time to include even the poorest Brazilians in the country's economy. The four already had an outline of the guiding principles to drive an innovative ten-year plan for economic prosperity.

"That Mercedes across the street – there's no one guarding it. Come on, comrades. Let's get it. It'll bring us a good price."

"Yeah. We can get dollars for it, not rubles."

"Okay. Let's go, Vlad, same as always. You get it unlocked; then you and Pavel look out for troublemakers. I'll get it started and drive. Let's go."

The owner of the Mercedes came out of the office of the Tverskaya travel agency, saw the three hoodlums coming, and dashed to get in his car and drive away. He didn't make it. And he would not be taking the trip he had just paid for.

"Look, Dimo. He was kind enough to unlock the door for us and leave us the keys."

"Good. Get in. Let's get going."

"Ah, listen to that motor. Beautiful."

"Stop admiring the motor, Dimo, and put it in gear."

"Wait – that woman. She's in our way."

"She's just standing there, staring at us."

"Honk the horn, Dimo, and just go!"

"Why doesn't she move? Get out of the way, woman."

"Go, Dimo!"

"I can't."

"What do you mean you can't? Step on it."

"I can't. I can't move. Vlad, I'm paralyzed. Look. I can't move my arms. My legs. I can't move anything."

"I don't believe it, Helge. Why are they saying she is the Christ? She doesn't say so."

"No, she says there are others like her. But she changes things, Solveig. They say everything in the city is changing."

"What's changing? The mayor of Moscow said 'hello' to her. What is that?"

"They say the streets are becoming quiet, the parliament has come to order, and crime is down – all in the past two weeks. They are talking about how her love changes everybody. Things are happening."

"Well, nothing is happening here in Barcelona, Helge. Look around. Do you see anything happening?" The warm Mediterranean breeze filtered softly through the columns of the Olympic esplanade, children laughed and scampered across the square paving stones, music of the sardana sounded faintly in the air. "Come on, my love. Get real."

"Maybe something is happening in Moscow," Solveig conceded. "But nothing like that is happening here. And nothing like that is happening back home in Oslo, is it? If Martin Luther were here, we could ask him. But he's not, and we're not in Moscow, and I'm not going to worry about it."

"Well, then, what about those reports on television. People all over the world are suddenly getting some flash of insight and then they take up some social cause, or devote their lives to the poor, or start a peacemaking movement."

"What's that got to do with Moscow?"

"Maybe nothing. But people are saying everything is related to her love. Her love connects us all."

"Connects us from Moscow?"

"Solveig, think of the timing. It has all been happening during the past two weeks – since she appeared. Already the whole world knows about it; the whole world knows her name."

"Yes, I've heard it - Nataliya Zolotaryov. Is that how you pronounce it?"

"You see, Solveig. You doubt, but you know her name."

"Ah, Helge, I don't want to even think about it. I just want to leave the rest of the world behind and enjoy our vacation. Let's relax and be peaceful and forget our Norwegian winter and just soak up the rays of this beautiful Spanish sun."

She started to lie back on the low parapet where they were sitting when, suddenly, the sky exploded.

"Helge!" she shrieked. She squeezed her eyes shut to shield them, clutched her husband's arm, and buried her head in the side of his chest. "What's happening?"

Helge had closed his eyes too and ducked his head into her hair. Now he slowly uncurled his head and shoulders and squinted up at the sky. "It's okay, Solveig. Look. Everything's normal."

She blinked open her eyes and looked around the esplanade. Indeed, it was just as it was before the explosion. Everyone was strolling about as though nothing had happened. However, deep within her being, she knew it was not as it was before – something really had happened.

"You did see that, didn't you Helge?"

"I don't know what I saw."

"We have things to do, Helge."

"Yes. I know." Helge took a notebook from his shirt pocket. Together they sketched a diagram of a retreat center in the mountains near Oslo where Nobel Peace Laureates could meet informally with world leaders to construct, esoterically, a planetary thoughtform around a campaign for world peace - to displace the thoughtform of war and violence. The two would build and support the center with funds they had earned in their business of developing and building scientific instruments.

A figure in the robes of an Eastern Orthodox priest emerged from the shadows and gently touched the arm of Nataliya Zolotaryov. "Madame," he whispered earnestly. "Please be careful. The Archbishop is denouncing you. He is turning the Church against you."

"And what is it that he is afraid of, my priest?"

"You are a woman, and therefore, he says, when people proclaim you to be the Christ it is a falsehood, and your teachings are a fraud. But most of all, you are not of the Church. He says you are nothing but a homeless beggar. Madame, we are forbidden to see you or speak about you. We are not allowed to believe in you."

"And what do you believe, my priest?"

"With my own eyes I see what you do, I see how people respond, and with my own heart I experience your love. I believe in you, my Lord. I am at your service."

"I am not the Christ, my priest. I am but one of the instruments of the Christ Impulse. There are many of us who have come among you, some with greater responsibility than others. Some you will see in public roles, others will be working behind the scenes and you won't notice them."

A puzzled look came over the priest's face. "What shall I . . . How shall I . . ."

"Believe in the Impulse, my priest. Believe in its mission of love, its objective of peace, its all-encompassing beauty, for we are all its servants, if we could only know it."

Ian glanced at his watch as he hurried to the Leicester Square tube station, warding off the cold February rain with a large black umbrella. He was late and he tried to move a little faster through the openings in the streaming sidewalk crowd. He knew Eva would have dinner waiting.

At the pedestrian crossing, he shifted his weight impatiently from one foot to the other, straining for the light to change to green. A navy blue Burberry brushed against his side and stepped blindly onto the road, into the traffic. The man's right hand clamped a phone to his ear, his left carried a newspaper and a briefcase. He had a large-brimmed bush hat which he had pulled low on his head. Ian saw the impending disaster and lunged into the traffic, grabbed the man around the chest, and literally threw him out of the street. The two of them tumbled back to the sidewalk.

As the two lay on the sidewalk trying to collect themselves, the ruffled Burberry blubbered out words of profuse thanks to Ian for saving his life, spouted a selection of curses at his own stupidity, and breathlessly exclaimed at how close he had come to death. People gathered around them and started to help them up. As Ian brushed off his slacks, he looked up and noticed, in the crowd of faces, one face that looked at him serenely, but purposefully. His whole being was vitalized. He immediately knew – intuitively – what the face represented. Then it seemed to disappear across the street just as a double-decker bus pulled up to the curb and cut off his view.

"Hello, Eva. I'm home," Ian called out, "and now I know my way to heaven."

"Home isn't heaven?" Eva questioned.

"Of course it is." He took her in his arms and kissed her.

"Mmm. Do that again," she whispered.

"I have something to tell you," he said as they released one another. "But first, I'd like us to spend some time in the meditation room. We are in a stream of purpose that needs our alignment." They sat in silence, their beings merging as one.

Afterward, Eva got out the candles for dinner and Ian spoke about his street adventure, describing, almost wordlessly but with a special quality of energy, his encounter with the face in the crowd. Eva needed few words – the energy said it all. She knew.

After dinner they talked about their preparations for the baby. "Ian, where shall we put the baby's bed? Here? Or over there?"

"If we put it here, we'll have room along the wall for his bookshelf."

"His bookshelf? Oh, I get it. For his biochemistry texts."

"No, for his philosophy books – a whole shelf for Plato and Aristotle."

"Very well, bookshelf it is. But he can choose his own books."

Ian wrapped his arms around his wife in a loving embrace, and passed his hand gently over her abdomen. Tears came to his eyes. "It's so incredibly wonderful, Eva, isn't it?"

"I know. I can hardly wait for him to be born. We've been pregnant just over three months and I'm beginning to feel as though I already know him. He is going to be a kind and gentle giant of a man, just like his father, and I will love him very much, just like I love his father."

He gave her a tender kiss. "Do you still like the name Nicholas?"

"Yes, I do, Ian. I think it suits him. Nicholas. You still like it, don't you? Nicholas Cameron. It sounds right, doesn't it? What do you think?"

"Sounds fine to me. What about a middle name? We won't give him any family names, will we?"

"No, let's just let him be whoever he will be."

"What about Edward. Is that too regal."

"Too abdicational. What about Anthony?"

"That would be Tony. Too Prime Ministerial."

"Right. Maybe we should wait for something brilliant. We still have six months to decide"

"Or have we?"

"What do you mean, Ian?"

"I mean, what if he wants an earlier - or later - astrological sign?"

"I'm sure early August is just what he wants."

Ian and Eva were supremely happy when they found out she was pregnant. From the beginning they had agreed on having a family as soon as they were married. Perhaps they were reacting to Ian's broken family; perhaps it was Eva's orphaned mother or her father's missing family – among Chile's disappeared; perhaps it was just the natural flow of their love. Both Ian and Eva saw that having children within their loving aura and nurturing them to maturity was a way of contributing to a better world.

Chapter Nineteen

Nicholas Cameron

It was August and Aiya waited patiently in Eva's room at the maternity home. Everything was happening right on schedule. It was during these final hours before delivery that Aiya began to make the first in a series of resonant connections to the body of the unborn baby. It was this beginning stage of its attachment to the baby that initiated the birth labor. At the moment of birth, Aiya would effect the final connection of its life aspect.

Ian had brought Eva to the maternity home early in the morning and the labor was progressing nicely, just like their pre-natal classes had predicted. In a few moments, the baby would be born and Aiya would become Nicholas as the baby uttered his first cry.

At almost the same time, Ohruu was getting ready to enter a physical form in a hospital maternity ward in Paris. The two souls were on the same incarnation theme, gathering with others in their group toward an earthly existence of service. They knew the personalities of the physical bodies they would inhabit would have no conscious awareness of the pre-incarnation pledge of service. However, Aiya and Ohruu would impress them with an inner urge toward alignment with the vast expression of love which had begun to embrace the planet. Their alignment would resonate as a coordinating influence and attract thought and action to the service intentions which Aiya and Ohruu had formulated.

Aiya and Ohruu knew also their intertwined incarnation themes would serve to meld their fields more completely, creating an even stronger unit in the service of the Impulse. Their personalities would have no conscious awareness of one another's existence and might never come together in the physical world – after all, they were going to two different countries. They would have to rely on the magnetic quality of their common vibration to strengthen the bond, a process that was space independent.

And now, the time had come. At the moment of delivery, Aiya lit the light of conscious life in the newborn baby, and Nicholas let out a cry.

Just as, six months earlier, the Christ had lit the light of a new life in humanity, and evoked the Thousand Awakenings.

Chapter Twenty

Jacqueline Garneau

"Madame Monique Garneau?"

"Oui."

The young woman extended her hand. "Madame Renée Lemieux." She forced a small smile. "De l'Administration Sociale."

"Bonjour." Madame Garneau leaned forward and shook hands. She frowned and tilted her head in curiosity.

"Madame, vous avez une fille . . . " She consulted her papers. "Your have a daughter, Michele Garneau?"

"Oui. Pourquoi?" Her eyebrows arched in question.

The young woman at the door hesitated, looking down at her feet.

"Why?" the mother insisted, now concerned. "What is it?"

"Votre fille, Madame. I am very sorry to tell you. Your daughter, Michele. She died this morning in Clinique Marceau."

"Non! Ce n'est pas possible. Michele, she is only twenty years old. Non. Non."

"I am very sorry, Madame. But it is true."

Madame Garneau shook her head in denial. Then, looking into the young woman's eyes, she saw the truth of the words. Her body sagged. She hid her face in her hands and cried deep wrenching tears. The younger woman held her, then helped her back into her flat and onto a couch. When Monique's sobbing had subsided, the woman began to explain.

"Madame, your daughter came into the hospital yesterday saying she felt very sick and was worried about the baby she was carrying."

"Baby? I did not even know she was pregnant. Oh, my poor Michele."

"Yes, Madame. She was very late in her ninth month. She said she had not seen you in more than a year. Her boyfriend left her and she was struggling to make it on her own – to prove she could do it. Like you did, she said."

"Oh, Mon Dieu. My poor, dear, little girl."

"Unfortunately, Madame, she had become very ill and by the time she came to us it was too late. It was all the doctors could do to save the child."

"They saved the child? I have a grandchild?"

"Yes, Madame. You have a granddaughter."

And so it was that Ohruu arrived in Paris right on schedule. After a week in the maternity ward, the doctors declared the baby was completely healthy and she was taken to the flat of her grandmother Monique. There she would be brought up with Monique and Monique's mother.

Monique Garneau lived on the edge of Parisian high society. A warmly sociable, handsome woman, she owned a highly efficient business which catered private parties for the rich and famous. In another part of her life, she was a successful fundraiser for a number of charities. Her friends said of her that, in her business, she could charm a smile out of a spider; in her fundraising, she could charm a franc out of a piece of coal. Now, she turned the love, which was the source of her charm, toward her newest enterprise – her granddaughter.

It had not been an easy life for Monique. Her father, Jacques Garneau, a young French Air Force officer, had been killed in a training exercise when she was a baby, and her mother had subsequently lived with three different men while Monique was growing up. As soon as she could, Monique started working as a waitress and then became a night club hostess. The unplanned birth of Michele ended that life and she started her catering business, enlisting friends as employees.

The business grew rapidly and Monique prospered. She bought a spacious flat in the fifth arrondissement in Paris where she and her daughter and her mother now lived in comfort. Monique's mother managed the accounting and administration for the business and helped to look after Michele. Monique attracted several suitors but she found no one she could love.

Michele's death dredged up an aching guilt which Monique thought she had successfully buried. In her attempt to protect her daughter from falling into the kind of life she herself had led in her late teens, Monique had tried to impose very strict boundaries on Michele's activities. She sent her to school at a conservative convent, she inspected her boyfriends critically, she imposed curfews and demanded an accounting of virtually all of Michele's waking hours. Inevitably, Michele rebelled, quit school, moved out of her mother's home and got a waitressing job, leaving her mother and her grandmother to worry constantly about her. Monique's worry turned to anger and then to guilt. Her attempts at reconciliation with Michele went nowhere and she eventually suppressed her guilt with a façade of acceptance and resignation.

The arrival of Michele's baby meant a second chance for Monique. This time, she would do it right. She would dispel her guilt through her devotion to her daughter's daughter. And that would not be hard, she thought, because as soon as she saw the baby, peering out from the hospital blanket, she knew they were made for each other. She named the child after her deceased father and declared she would be the perfect mother for little Jacqueline.

Chapter Twenty-One

Nicholas and Jacqueline

Eva Cameron was the only child of Martine and Carlos Rivera, so Nicholas Cameron was their only grandchild. The baby reached up to his grandmother and Martine took him gently into her arms. Nicholas was two months old and this was his first meeting with his maternal grandparents.

Nicholas' other grandfather, Mac Cameron, was careful not to intrude. He could appreciate how much Martine wanted to hold her grandchild. The baby was precious to them all. He considered himself fortunate to be living in London and able to spend a lot of time with Ian and Eva and their baby. Now it was the turn of Martine and Carlos to get to know Nicholas.

"Nicholas, my darling," Martine cooed at the baby as she cuddled him. "Look at him smile, Carlos," she said, holding him before her husband. "Look how happy he is." Her eyes glittered with tears of love.

Mac remembered his own tears the first time he saw the baby just a few hours after he was born. He was especially touched when Eva handed the tiny bundle to him to hold. That was when the tears had come to his own eyes, tears which had not surprised him – he knew the joyous reaction of soul meeting soul. Now he saw how the new little life had generated an aura of well being in Martine, opening her to the beauty and the power of love.

"Look at his eyes, Carlos, and his smile. Isn't our grandson handsome? I think he looks like you."

"Martine, for goodness sake. He is just a baby. Don't inflict him with my looks already."

Mac smiled wryly. The baby's dark hair was certainly not from the Cameron side of the family, but the blue eyes were.

"Here, Carlos, you hold him."

"Come here, hombre," Carlos said happily, and hoisted Nicholas up over his head. "Olé! Olé!" he cried, tossing him gently. "Fly, Nickie. Fly." The baby gurgled a squeal and giggled.

"Carlos!" Martine scolded. "Be careful. Eva and Ian will send us back to Paris."

"Then we'll take Nickie with us." Carlos laughed and tossed the baby up in the air again. "Okay hombre?"

Carlos and Martine had come from Paris that morning to see their grandchild. Only two days earlier they had arrived back in Paris from Ecuador. They had spent most of the last five years working on behalf of the poorest communities in Ecuador, Peru and Bolivia. Carlos Rivera was a journalist and wrote articles for several international publications calling attention to the conditions of poverty in those countries, and making the case for political action and diplomatic pressure to effect needed changes. Martine was a nurse. She had set up medical clinics in remote areas and trained local women to provide their neighbors with basic health care education.

The two had come to their work for the poor from different directions. Carlos had escaped the death squads in Chile after his father and older brother disappeared. He made his way to France where he began to write about social problems, using his mastery of Spanish, French, and English to reach several foreign audiences. Martine was raised by nuns in an orphanage in Normandy. After training as a public health nurse she worked in the poorest arrondissements in Paris. They met at a street protest for the homeless that had gathered outside the exclusive Tour d'Argent restaurant. Carlos was an enthusiastic intellectual idealist. Martine was the practical one with a sensitive charm that endeared her to everyone she met. She backed her charm with tireless persistence that wore people down until they agreed to her requests.

"Eva, you must let me take him for a walk, as soon as you have fed him. You want to go for a walk, don't you Nicholas? See, Eva? He wants to go."

"Mama, he has to have a nap after his feeding. Then he can go."

"Et bien, mon pettit. After your nap."

Grandpa Mac remained in the background, watching his grandson being absorbed by the other grandparents. His heart went out to all of them.

"Jacqueline, Jacqueline, sweetheart, please don't cry. Look, Mama. Her temperature is very high. I am not waiting any longer. I am taking her to the doctor."

"Monique, she's a baby. You know babies get high temperatures. It's probably nothing serious."

"I don't care. I'm not taking any chances."

Of course it was nothing serious and the fever subsided within a few hours. As the weeks went by, Monique continued to keep a close watch on every possible symptom of a health problem and treated every little bump and bruise as a potential disaster. Jacqueline was a wiry, active little girl with an adventuresome spirit, so there were many trips to the doctor. When Jacqueline started to walk, Monique was quick to pick her up when she stumbled. When she was five, she fell off a park swing and badly scraped her knee. Monique rushed her to the doctor for treatment – which needed only a gentle washing of the wound.

"Monique, you have to let her get a few bumps and bruises. You have to let her learn to look after herself." Monique's mother nagged constantly to get her daughter to let Jacqueline grow up normally. "Being a perfect parent doesn't mean protecting the child from life. Give it a break, Monique. Relax. She is a sturdy young lady soon to start school. You have to let go."

"I know, Mama. It's just that . . ."

"It's just that you think you didn't get it right with Michele. Well, don't you see, dear? You are on the same path with Jacqueline. She needs to be free to learn. And you, my dear, you need to be free to live your own life again. Since Jacqueline arrived, you have not taken a single day for yourself. Six years without a holiday. That's not right."

"But Mama . . ."

"No buts, Monique. Look, the business is quiet in the summer. Why don't you go away for a couple of weeks and leave Jacqueline with me? Call it a sabbatical – a retreat. Use the time to find yourself again. We'll be just fine."

"Could you really manage, Mama?"

"Come now. I may be sixty-five years old but I am hardly decrepit. Jacqueline and I will have a ball. Just the two of us. You go. And don't worry for one minute. Pack your bags and go."

The train ride from Paris to London to Torquay in Devon, England, was decompression time for Monique. The area known as the English Riviera was a tourist center, but now in late June things were still relatively quiet. Monique had spent several weeks here as a teenager attending one of the many language schools in company with students from all over Europe. It was the good memories of those days which had brought her back.

She chose a suite in a private hotel overlooking the beach. It was cozy and quiet and the sea air was a welcome change from the summer stuffiness of Paris. As soon as she reached her room, even before she looked out the window to check the view, she was dialing back to Paris to speak with Jacqueline. Her mother put the six-year-old on the telephone immediately. Monique listened attentively to the child's delightfully enthusiastic stories of her day. The anxiety of her separation from the child quickly evaporated in the midst of Jacqueline's happy laughter.

Next morning, after an early breakfast on the verandah, Monique strolled down to the bay, along the promenade, and then through the shops in town. A lot had changed in the town center over thirty years – more bars, more entertainment arcades, more fast food outlets, more traffic. Her mind chattered with comparisons, with memories of her teenage years, with thoughts of home, with analysis of restaurant menus – anything that would avoid dealing with her mother's admonition to find herself again. She was afraid of what she might find – or not find.

She wandered on through the town and up the hill away from the bay, choosing streets randomly. These streets of residences and small hotels had changed much less. She occupied her mind with naming flowers which hung over stone walls and reading quaint advertising signs at the front of the hotels along the way. It was a warm, breezy morning with intermittent sun shining through the scattered clouds. Monique decided she was enjoying the walk - it was good for her, she affirmed.

For no conscious reason she paused at the steps leading to a side door of a small Anglican church. She hadn't been in any church since childhood. Why was she stopping here? She hesitated only a moment, then walked down the steps and through the door into the church. It wasn't the religion she had been brought up in, but there she was, and it seemed alright for her to be there. It is quietly beautiful, she thought, as she gazed around the interior - not too elaborate.

She stepped slowly and gently toward the altar. Her childhood training flooded back as she knelt and crossed herself and mouthed the ritual words. How many long years had it been since she had last done that? She stepped into a side pew and sat down, trying to orient herself to her surroundings. Briefly, she questioned why she had come into the church but she quickly ignored the question and started to examine the church's architecture and decorations. Here and there she saw several elements she might be able to incorporate in table and room arrangements in her catering business. Her mind was busy analyzing, speculating, making mental notes.

A bright flash of sunlight pierced a stained glass window to her right and caught the corner of her eye. She looked up and followed the probing ray to a golden sculpture of an eagle standing to the left of the pulpit. The eagle glowed brightly for a few moments and she stared intently at it. Then a cloud covered the sun again. In that flash, Monique felt a physical body shift. Her gaze softened, her mind dropped into neutral, her shoulders relaxed. She drew a deep breath, then let it out with a long sigh. Her head dropped onto her chest and she broke into tears. Then she heard the inner words, "You are in the arms of God," and she gave in, this woman of the world. She let go of her fight to sustain the public mask of success. Something new could now give her strength.

After some minutes in the silence of utter bliss, her mind awoke to the sudden intrusion of a disturbing stream of thoughts: *Where have I been all of these forty-six years of my life? Struggling, struggling- lost in the struggle – for what? For what purpose?* She left the church, the peace of the golden eagle having given way to the emotion of self-doubt. She headed for the road which she knew would take her to the wooded trail along the cliffs. She had found solace there as a teenager; maybe she could find it again.

Her street shoes were not the best for this trail but she trudged along with heavy steps and heavy heart to an opening in the trees that looked out on the ocean. She looked down and watched the wind-born waves crash and roil among the rocks below. It was mesmerizing. It gave her the feeling her emotions were being tumbled and washed. She closed her eyes and shut out the noise of the surf. When she opened them, she looked up and out, above the sea, into infinite space. Her past, her present, her future drifted back and forth through her consciousness. Her future became quiet. Her memories of the past dimmed. She gave way to the now. She began to find herself.

Every August for the next ten years, Monique returned to Torquay for a vacation and took her mother and Jacqueline with her. Their days followed a comfortable routine – sunning on the broad sandy beach when there was sun, touring southwest England when there were clouds, enjoying clotted cream and strawberry jam at afternoon tea, and frequenting their favorite restaurants for dinner. Monique's mother especially liked the local apple cider and often had plaice for dinner. Little Jacqueline liked to hang around the older language students who gathered in the park to play football and volleyball. She had a maturity and intelligence beyond her years, so they often included her in their conversations. Early each morning Monique found her pew in the little Anglican church, and on many days she walked on the cliffs alone.

Another Torquay routine was Jacqueline's birthday party. Monique invited the cluster of children which Jacqueline's bright sociability attracted when they were playing on the beach. They took over a section of one of the restaurants and Monique applied her catering creativity to make these memorable events. As Jacqueline entered her teens, the parties became more sophisticated and shifted from lunches and afternoons to dinners and evenings.

At Jacqueline's seventeenth birthday dinner, Monique's mother whispered, "Enjoy this, Monique. She has grown up. This will probably be the last summer she'll want to spend her vacation with us."

Monique only half heard her mother. Something else had her attention. "Mama, who is that boy she's sitting beside?"

"I don't know. I think he's English, but listen - he speaks French like a Parisian."

Chapter Twenty-Two

A Youthful Nicholas

"Hello? Is that you, Nicholas?"

"Yes. Oh, hello Dad."

"Nicholas, the Headmaster just called."

Nick pressed his lips together in annoyance, then relaxed them in resignation. He had spent a half-hour with the Headmaster that morning, listening to an evaluation of his academic performance. "You could do so much better, Nicholas," the Headmaster had admonished. "You could be at the head of the class. You must apply yourself young man." Now, Nick realized, the Headmaster had enrolled his father in the cause. He waited for his father's next words.

"Do you hear, Nicholas?"

"Yes, father."

"Your mother and I are worried, Nick. You have to apply to Cambridge soon and they will want better grades than these last ones you produced. Shall we come there this weekend? Or will you come to London? We need to talk about this Nick."

"Dad, I'm going to Paris for the weekend."

"Paris? Is it your football team? I didn't hear about it."

"No, it's . . . I am going to see a friend."

"A friend? Who?"

"A friend I met last summer. Her mother has invited me. We are going to go to the opera."

"*Her* mother? Whose mother? Nicholas, what's going on?"

"Yes, Madame Garneau, I have to say my parents are concerned about my coming here. They think I should be studying so I can get into Cambridge. Like my father - and my grandfather."

"Ah, Nicholas. I should have spoken to them before I invited you."

"Perhaps. But then they might have said 'no,' and I would have come anyway, and that would have been worse for them."

"But, Nicholas, maybe they are right and you should be studying."

"Oh, I'll be fine, Madame Garneau. If I decide I want to go to Cambridge, I think they will accept me – my grades are not that bad. And they'll count all the other things as well – my athletics, my debating, maybe the other things I do."

"Mama, he helps at a child care center in a church - as a volunteer. And he teaches swimming to some handicapped kids." Jacqueline bounced as she spoke and hugged his arm, which she had been clinging to since they met him at the heliport. Nicholas noted she called Monique 'Mama' even though Monique was Jacqueline's grandmother.

"Still, Nicholas," Monique persisted, "I'm sure your parents are just wishing the best for you."

"Oh, I know they are. But maybe I don't want to study where my father and grandfather did. Maybe I'll go to a university in America. Or to the Sorbonne. Or I'll get a job – I bet my grandfather can get me a job in the Foreign Service. Or I'll travel. I can't decide my whole future when I'm only seventeen years old. I need to try different things before I can know what is right for me. A lot of people do very well without going to Cambridge or Oxford."

Jacqueline squeezed Nicholas' arm and said, "I can see you are so clear about your life, my Nicholas. You know exactly what you are going to do." She grinned and pulled him closer.

"Well, I don't want to shut any doors."

"Still," Monique pressed, "I'm sorry I didn't speak to your parents before inviting you. I'll call them now and apologize, shall I?"

"No. Thank you Madame Garneau. I can explain everything to them. It's just my grades they are worried about."

"Et bien, mes enfants. We have time for a walk before dinner and the opera house. Would you like that?"

"Madame Garneau, isn't that where Le Tour d'Argent restaurant is?" Nicholas pointed to the building at the end of bridge they were crossing.

"Why, yes it is, Nicholas. On the top floor."

"This must be where my grandmother Martine says she met my Papa Carlos. That was more than forty years ago."

"They met at a dinner party?" Monique asked.

"Heavens no. They met in the street. Right about here, I guess. They were part of a protest for poor people."

"Do they live here in Paris now?"

"They do when they're not living somewhere else. Right now they are in Mozambique helping to build a new hospital. They're almost seventy now, and still working for the poor."

Jacqueline pulled at Nicholas' arm and said, "I'll bet you would like to work for the poor, wouldn't you Nicholas. You told me in Torquay about the time you took all your clothes to that poor family."

"Not all my clothes."

"And I saw you give your rain jacket to that man outside the cathedral in Exeter."

"He was cold and wet. He needed it more than I did."

"Do you often do that sort of thing, Nicholas?"

"Well, Madame Garneau, I see these people with nothing and I look at everything I have and I feel compelled to do something. Maybe that's why I'm not

138

too concerned about Cambridge. There seem to be so many other things in the world that are more important than being known as a graduate of Cambridge."

"What do you think about that, Jacqueline?" Monique realized she and her daughter had never spoken about such things.

"Mama, I think the same thing when I work at those fabulous parties you cater – the food, the wine, the decorations, all the elaborate, showy jewelry that the people wear. And their clothes – some of those gowns are worth a fortune. And right outside on the street are people without enough food for a day."

"I didn't know you thought that way, sweetheart."

"I know it's your business, Mama," she went on, "and it's what gives me everything I have, so I'm not ungrateful, and I do appreciate the opportunity to work there and earn some money, and you do such a perfect job." Jacqueline was trying to exclude Monique from her critique of the lifestyles of the wealthy. "But Mama, how can people spend all that money on all that – you know - unimportant nothing? There is such a distance between the rich and the poor. It's not fair, Mama. And I know you think about it too - you raise all that money for your charities."

"Maybe your mother is Robin Hood, Jacqueline. She has figured out how to take it from the rich and give it to the poor." He squeezed her hand.

"Here it is Nicholas - your letter from the Cambridge admissions office. They still don't use a communicator for such matters."

"Thanks, Dad. Nick opened the envelope and read aloud. "Dear Mr. Cameron, We are sorry to inform you that . . ." He didn't have to read further.

"Well, that's it," his father said, and abruptly left the room. His mother put her arm around Nick's shoulder, saying, "Well, it worked out alright, didn't it Nicholas dear? Your father's school is not what you wanted, and now you can do what you want." She gave him a hug.

"In a little while our son will be gone, Ian. Are you ready to let him go?"

"No problem, Eva. I am proud of him and pleased for him. He has begun to define his own life. After all these years of encouraging him to think for himself, what more could we ask? He is eighteen years old – it is time for him to be independent. It's time for him to strike out on his own."

"You're not disappointed in his failure to be admitted to Cambridge?"

"You know I was at first. But I quickly got over it. He'll do just fine."

"I'm sure he will, dear. Still, I am worried about his plan – rather, his lack of plan. He says he's going traveling but he doesn't know where or how."

"He says he's going to Paris first. To see that girl. What's her name?"

"Jacqueline. Jacqueline Garneau. He says he has to say good bye. But then what? He hasn't told me anything else. Has he told you what he's going to do next?"

"He doesn't know. He says he'll decide each day what to do next. He will get whatever jobs he can find because he's not taking very much money with him. Only enough for a few weeks."

"Oh, Ian. He could wind up on the street or something."

"He could, but he won't. Not our Nicholas. I don't worry about him Eva. He's smart, he's resourceful, and he's strong and healthy. He can take care of himself."

"All he told me was he wants to see the world. The world's a very big place. Where could he be going?"

"He'll have his communicator with him, Eva. He'll keep in touch."

"Yes, I know he will. I know he'll communicate every day with his little sister. Have you noticed how he and Gwynneth are very close now?"

"He still looks after her, doesn't he? And, by the way, she's not so little any more, Eva. She'll be seventeen next month."

"They grow up quickly, don't they Ian?"

"Jacqueline, this is hard. But I have to say it clearly. I am going to Marseilles and I will try to get a job on a cruise ship. I will go wherever it goes. I don't know where that will be, or what I will do after that."

"But Nicholas . . . why?"

"This is something I just have to do. I don't know what it is I am searching for, but something is driving me. For your sake, you have to forget I ever existed because I cannot promise when – or even if - I will ever be back. You have to get on with your life. I'm not saying 'a bientôt', Jacqueline. For your sake, it has to be 'good-bye'."

"Nicholas, are you sure?"

Chapter Twenty-Three

Resonance Revisited

The display of tropical blossoms in the florist's window caught Nicholas' eye as he hurried toward the South Kensington tube station. The flowers reminded him of his ship's stopover in Malaysia more than three and a half years before - the flowers in the tropics were overwhelmingly beautiful, he remembered. He stopped to admire the florist's window, stepping under the awning to shelter from the rain shower which had sprung up suddenly on what had been a sunny afternoon.

The bouquet of large lily-like flowers at the back was especially attractive. Perhaps he would buy it for his mother, he thought. Then as his focus shifted, he noticed a face reflected in the window, the face of a young woman standing beside him.

He stared at the reflection. Could it be her? "Jacqueline?" he asked, catching his breath as he spoke.

The young woman turned. Her eyes widened in disbelief. "Nicholas?" Jacqueline was shocked. It had happened. She had had a strange premonition she would meet him on this visit to London, but hadn't let herself believe it.

They stared at each other for a moment, each searching the others' eyes, trying to take in where they stood with one another. Finally, Jacqueline held out both her hands and Nicholas took them in his.

142

"It is so good to see you, Nicholas. Are you living here again?"

"Yes. I've been back a little more than a year. I'm at Cambridge. Reading philosophy. And you? What are you doing here in London?" Her French accent is barely detectable, he noted, and she is just as pretty as ever. "Are you studying here?"

"I've been visiting my friend, Carole. We were at school together in Paris and now she is studying at the London School of Economics. I was just looking at these flowers, deciding which ones to get her as a thank-you gift. I'm going back to Paris tomorrow morning."

"Oh." A flicker of anxiety caught him in the solar plexus. "Do you have time for a cup of coffee? Or tea? There's a very nice tea room just around the corner."

She hesitated, unsure of her own feelings. Then, "That would be nice."

There was a curious tension between them as they sipped their tea. Nicholas was bursting to hold her and smother her with kisses, but held himself in check. Jacqueline could feel his restrained energy and tried to defuse it with a cool correctness. "It has been more than three years, hasn't it Nicholas, since you left on your quest. I guess a lot has happened to you. Where have you been? What have you been doing?"

"Well, I did get the job with the cruise company and worked on three different ships. First in the Med. Then some runs through the Suez to the Far East and Australia and New Zealand. Then across to America. I was a waiter for the first six months. Then I was a passenger service representative – a kind of host, looking after the passengers' every wish. I really enjoyed doing that job."

"Did you find what you went looking for Nicholas?"

He shook his head. "Well, no. It was . . . No. . . I didn't. I'm still searching. It's really frustrating." He rearranged the silverware in front of him, then looked up at her and smiled. "But I did find a better place to look," he said, pointing to his chest. "In here." He wondered whether to tell her more about himself. He wanted to, but thought better of it. "And what about you, Jacqueline? How have you been?"

"I've been very happy." She had to exert herself to say those words in his presence. "I've been with Jean Claude for over a year now. We're both at the Sorbonne and we get along very well."

Ah, so that's it. Well, what did you expect, Nicholas? Did you think she would enter a convent? He took a breath and smiled weakly. "So, you're happy with your studies too?" *Is she really happy with Jean Claude? Was there a hesitation in her voice?*

"Oh, very much so." She saw his disappointment and felt his energy dim. "I'm in my third year, learning the new psychology – you've probably heard about it. It's based on the seven rays and the chakras."

He came alive again. "That's brilliant. Please tell me. What are you learning?"

"Do you know about these things?"

"My parents spoke about chakras and energies all the time, although I can't say I took in much of it. Then, the ship's engineer taught me a lot about the physics of light and sound and about particle physics. He said I should think about physics in relation to the human energy system. I think he must have read everything ever written about quantum mechanics. Or, so it seemed to me. But you are doing psychology and energies. Please. Tell me about it."

There was a spark of connection which flashed between them as he spoke. Her chin tilted up slightly, an unconscious response to the spark. Without thinking, she touched his hand. As she started to reply to his question she looked down and saw the touch, and pulled her hand back. "The premise is simple," she explained, self-consciously at first, in the memory of the touch to his hand. Then, more freely, "Our thoughts and our emotions are substances of energy and our lives, our actions, are impulsed by those substances. There are certain waves of universal energy impulses – the seven rays, they are called – which each qualify our energy fields in particular ways. The chakras are action centers within our energy fields which transmit these impulses to our physical being – our external selves." She spoke matter-of-factly with a direct, clear demeanor, as though teaching from a comprehensive ownership of her facts.

He could discuss these things with her forever, he thought. "So, our behavior is all about how the energies are impulsing us?"

"Yes, and what energies are flowing, and where they are restricted or excessive, and where they are focused."

He frowned in concentration as he tried to comprehend. "Fascinating." His mind scurried with connections to other mental frameworks. "Here, more tea?" he offered.

"Thank you."

"And so," he reasoned aloud, "psychological assessments are based on assessments of all the different energy qualities and flows in the individual?" Nicholas pursued the subject intently, forgetting for the moment the touch of her hand.

"And also the level of maturity," Jacqueline added, "maturity being the degree to which the individual has learned to handle these energies, has learned to tune to their higher vibration frequencies."

"Higher frequencies. It sounds like the physics I've been studying."

"I thought you were reading philosophy."

"I am. It includes religion." Her vitality was even more joyful than he remembered it. "And now that

145

religion and science are overlapping, I'm reading a lot of science – especially physics - quantum mechanics. My best friend at Cambridge is a physicist. And your psychology sounds like physics."

"Well, indeed it is physics. It is very real. We can measure these energy flows scientifically and relate them to our behavior. We can also correlate them with the condition of our physical bodies. When we refine the energy fields, we improve the mental, emotional, and physical health of the human being. We are talking about a new medicine as well as a new psychology."

"Medicine and psychology - it makes sense. The Greek word, 'psyche,' means soul, or principle of life. Refine the energies to heal – to help us express the perfection of soul. That's what my Grandpa Mac talks about."

"People have been working with human energy fields for thousands of years. What's new is we are working with much more complexity than before, and we have a broad scientific foundation and objective measurements to support our theories."

They huddled over their tea for more than an hour, Jacqueline elaborating on her studies, Nicholas listening and questioning and summarizing. She suddenly withdrew from the conversation to look at her watch. "Oh, Nicholas. Look at the time. I must go. I still have to buy the flowers for Carole."

"Yes, of course."

"Thank you for the tea, Nicholas. It has been good to see you." They stood and looked at one another for a moment without speaking. Then she gathered up her jacket and purse. "Good luck with your studies at Cambridge." She held out her hand formally, and with reluctance, he responded just as formally. She preceded him to the door and he watched her hurry down the street and disappear into the crowd.

"She is so beautiful, Gwyn," Nicholas had stopped at his sister's flat and was relating his encounter with Jacqueline. He and Gwynneth had become even closer since he returned from his travels, but with a twist – now it was she who seemed to be looking after him, at least emotionally. "She is so petite, Gwyn, yet seems so strong. Her eyes – she has big, bright gray-green eyes, and soft auburn hair. And her smile – her smile is like a beautiful sonata." And the brief touch of her hand – he didn't mention that to his sister, but it is what he remembered most. "And smart. She's about the most intelligent person I've ever met."

"You're smitten, my worldly brother. Absolutely smitten." Gwynneth laughed and threw a cushion at him as he slumped in anguish in the corner of the sofa.

"I'm so in love with her, Gwyn. But then, who wouldn't be?"

"So get with it, Nick. What are you going to do about it?"

"There's nothing I can do about it, is there. She's living with this Jean Claude guy."

"You said you didn't believe her when she said she was happy."

"I just thought she was a little unenthusiastic. But maybe that was how I wanted to hear it."

"And maybe you had better find out if you are the one who will make her enthusiastically happy."

"Ah, Gwyn. It's useless." He pounded his fist into the pillow. "If she says she's happy, who am I to say she's not."

"Oh, Jackie. Thank you so much. These white orchid stems are gorgeous. Thank you, thank you."

"You're very welcome, Carole." The two former schoolmates hugged one another.

"When you visited me two years ago, you brought me those beautiful big white tropical blossoms. Now these."

"I remembered how you like white flowers, Carole." Jacqueline remembered everything about that day two years earlier.

"I do. They are so pure."

"So much has happened for you since then, Carole." Jacqueline took both of Carole's hands in hers. "You've completed your doctorate, you have a post-doc research position, and now you are getting married. How wonderful."

"It is wonderful, isn't it. And now you arrive - it is so sweet of you to come early to help me get ready for the wedding, Jackie. I am so grateful. You really are my best friend."

"I wouldn't miss your wedding."

"Well, we both may miss it if I don't get everything done. Let me put my dress on and you can help me with the fit."

"Sure." While she waited for her friend to put on the dress, Jacqueline looked around Carole's room to see what had changed since her last visit. She picked up a photograph from the dressing table. "Carole, who are all these people? The ones in this photo. It looks like a party in a pub." Jacqueline examined the snapshot framed in a simple plastic holder.

"That's what it is. We were celebrating the end of our university years and trying to avoid thinking about real life. Didn't you and your classmates at the Sorbonne do something like that when you graduated?"

"Some of us did. These are all classmates of yours?"

"Mostly. A couple of the girls brought boyfriends. Here, Jackie, help me into my dress, will you please?"

Jacqueline put the picture back on the dressing table and helped Carole wiggle into her wedding dress. They needed to give it just a final tuck and gather. As Jacqueline did up the row of buttons at the back, she kept looking over at the photo. She focused particularly on one of the men at the back of the crowd, his face partly obscured by the waving hand of the girl in the front row. Could it be him?

Carole stood before the mirror. "Look, Jackie, it just needs a little taking in at the waist, don't you think? Can you pin it?"

Jacqueline forced herself to concentrate on the dress. She pulled the material in with four pins. "There, that should do it."

"Thanks, Jackie." Carole swirled around to flare the skirt. "How does it look?"

"Carole, it's beautiful. Wait. A little from the hip." In spite of herself, Jacqueline's mind remained on the photo as she worked with the alterations.

"There. How's that?"

"That's perfect, Jackie. Now, the hem."

As Jacqueline knelt down to pin the hem, she asked, "Carole, the two men at the back of the photo – they don't seem to be a part of the group. Are they the boyfriends?"

"Where? Oh yeah. Well, the one on the left is. The one on the right – I don't know him. Sally brought him but he is not her boyfriend. She says he's 'England's Most Eligible Bachelor.' Beautiful guy - sensitive, athletic, intelligent – the women all love him but nobody can hook him. Sally said something about him pining for a long lost love or something. Can you get the hem even, Jackie, with all those folds?"

Jacqueline buried her face in the flowing fabric as she fumbled with the pins. "I think I can." She began to feel anxious for Carole's wedding to be over so she could get away from London. She wanted to get back to Jean Claude. She blinked her eyes to stop a tear. Or is that really what she wanted? "Ouch!" She pricked her finger with a pin.

Nicholas pointed with his glass of fruit spritzer toward the bridge that spanned the River Cam. "It's like that bridge, Lloyd, connecting two quite different sides of the same river. You and I - as different as chalk and cheese – yet somehow strongly connected around a common flow of life." Nicholas and his friends often met at the pub by the lock and took their drinks outside where they discussed the affairs of the world. It was an important part of their Cambridge experience. Lloyd Williams was his best friend. They would both graduate in a month with the class of 2030.

"We're different, true enough, Nick."

"You heard my Grandfather Mac say he could tell we were from the same soul group."

"How could he tell?"

"My grandfather knows, Lloyd. He just seems to know." Nicholas and his grandfather had been very close all through Nicholas' life. "He knows - not in the way you and I say we know something. With him it's different. He says he connects with what he calls Universal Intelligence, where the truth of everything exists. He and I have talked about it since I was a small boy. It's a different way of knowing about things - a special kind of intuition. He says more and more people are on to it."

"Well, he may know but I would like to see some evidence. Like, this stone wall we are sitting on – I know how it was built. That river lock – I know how it works."

"Okay, scientist, but the behavior of sub-atomic particles - do you know how that works?"

"We have theories."

"Right. Then let's look at some evidence for my grandfather's theory. For three generations, your family has been born in Cardiff and mine in London. No connecting links, right? You went to grammar school there and I went to residence school in Essex. Our paths never crossed. You are at King's College and I am at Emmanuel, you are reading physics and I am reading philosophy. You call yourself a scientific entrepreneur and you call me a religious philosopher. You play chess, I play rugby. Nothing in common, okay?"

"Okay."

"So, think about it. The first time we meet is in the discussion session after Professor O'Connor's lecture on how we could all promote world peace. That was one month ago. How come we both wind up there? Among the fifty or so people in the discussion, you and I have our own conversation. How come? For all the differences in our backgrounds, how come, in just two hours there, we discovered we share views on world affairs, we share an urge to help people in need, and we share an interest in exploring the Ancient Wisdom. Then we discover we can read one another's thoughts. Now we both say we don't have closer friends. The connection between us was immediate, Lloyd, and intense. Explain all that scientifically."

"Coincidence, Nick. The law of probabilities."

"And the common bond we sometimes feel? Coincidence?"

"Maybe. Maybe not."

The next morning, in his room above his college's tranquil inner courtyard, Nicholas sat at the window and let his eyes wander along the pattern of the garden beds below as he let his mind wander through his conversation with Lloyd. Inevitably, it wandered right into those compelling thoughts about his connection with Jacqueline. As if on cue, his heart filled, his breathing stopped, and he was with her. It was happening more often these days. If he were still eighteen, he might put these occurrences down to adolescent infatuation. But at twenty-four? After two and a half years at sea and nearly four years of university? Impulsively, he picked up his communicator and contacted his Nana Rivera in Paris.

" 'Allo, oui?"

"Nana, it's Nicholas."

"Nicholas! Mon enfant. How are you? When are you coming to see us?"

"What about this coming weekend, Nana?"

"Perfect. Papa Carlos is arriving home tomorrow, so he will be here too."

"Wonderful. I haven't seen him for almost a year. Can we have dinner out on Saturday night – my treat?"

"Of course, but not your treat. Not in Paris, mon enfant."

"What is it Jacqueline? What's the matter?"

"Mon Dieu, Mama!" Jacqueline had stopped and held Monique by the arm. "Mama, look." Monique followed Jacqueline's gaze to the cluster of sidewalk dinner tables in front of the bistro.

"Near the back, Mama. It's him. It's Nicholas. Oh, Mama, what shall I do?"

"Well, I don't know what you are going to do, my dear, but I am going to go to their table and say 'hello' to him."

Jacqueline literally danced along behind Monique as they approached Nicholas and his grandparents. "Good evening, Nicholas. Do you remember me?" Monique asked. "It has been a few years."

"Why, Madame Garneau. Of course." Nicholas jumped to his feet. "And Jacqueline. Hello! This is wonderful. Nana, Papa, I would like you to meet Madame Garneau and her daughter Jacqueline. Madame, Jackie, these are my grandparents, Monsieur et Madame Rivera." They shook hands all round.

"Please call me Monique."

"And we are Martine and Carlos. You will join us for dinner, please?" Carlos looked for the waiter. "Garçon. Deux chaises, s'il vous plait."

"Oh, really. We mustn't intrude."

"Not at all. You are not intruding. We just got here ourselves. Please." Carlos was insistent. The waiter brought the extra chairs and Jacqueline slipped around behind Monique in order to sit next to Nicholas.

"So, Nickie!" Carlos exclaimed in his most exuberant voice. "This must be the famous Jacqueline you have been going on about." Nicholas squirmed and smiled lamely while beside him Jacqueline beamed.

"Carlos!" Martine poked him sharply in the ribs with an elbow. "Don't embarrass the boy."

"Look at him, Martine." He laughed heartily. "He has the face of a man in love."

"Carlos!"

"Alright, I apologize, Nickie," Carlos laughed, quite unapologetically. Carlos had immediately sized up the situation and knew exactly what he was doing. "But I am a journalist," he continued. "I have to get all the facts, you know. And it is my job to spread the news." He laughed again, at the same time stroking his wife's hand to placate her.

"Don't mind him, Jacqueline," Martine said soothingly. "We are very pleased to meet you."

"Thank you, Madame Rivera," Jacqueline responded, completely unruffled by Carlos. In fact she was excited at hearing the news the journalist had just broadcast. "I remember seeing you with Nicholas in Torquay many years ago and it is a pleasure to see you again."

"Now, that's done," Carlos announced. "It is time to order. What shall we have?"

By the time the food arrived, Monique and the Riveras were caught up in conversation as though they had been friends for years. Nicholas and Jacqueline ate in silence, seemingly keeping apart from the others, and apart from one another, each unable to start the conversation for fear of misspeaking.

"Don't be your usual impulsive self," Nicholas said to himself. "You always act without thinking. Don't do that now or you'll blow it."

"It is too sudden," Jacqueline said to herself. "You have to let things soak in for a while."

The silence continued as they poked at their food. Finally, Jacqueline could stand it no longer. She put her knife and fork down and put both her hands around Nicholas' upper arm, leaned close to him and whispered in his ear, "Je t'aime. Je t'aime Nicholas. I love you."

Aiya and Ohruu had come together.

Chapter Twenty-Four

The Wedding

"Gwynneth? Are you home?" Nicholas called up and downstairs, hoping his sister would be at their parent's home – she often stayed with them. He wanted to tell her all about Jacqueline, and about their plans. He called again. "Gwyn?" No answer.

It would be another three hours before his parents would be home so Nicholas left a note for them and caught the Flyer back to Cambridge. On the way, he called Lloyd Williams and asked him to meet him at the pub by the lock. "I'll be there by six, Lloyd. Can you make it? It's important." Lloyd wanted to know what it was about, and Nicholas could not hold back his news. "It's Jackie. We're getting married." He waited for Lloyd's reaction, then laughing at his friend's retort, repeated, "Yes, married!"

"It should be just our closest friends and relatives, Nick, don't you think?"

"Yes, Love. Let's make it quiet and intimate."

"And beautiful. It must be beautiful in every way, Nick.

"Of course, Jackie. Beauty will reign. So, which friends?"

"Well, for me, just Carole. She's my closest friend, and she lives here in London."

"And for me, just Lloyd."

"You know, Nick, since Grandmaman died, Mama is my only relative."

Nicholas put his arm around her and said, "Soon you'll have many more, Jackie."

"I'm looking forward to it mon amour – to being part of a larger family."

"So, there's my Grandpa Mac, Nana and Papa Rivera, and my parents, and Gwynneth."

"And Lisa, Nick, what about your Aunt Lisa - would she come from New York? And your Great Aunt Patricia in Australia?"

"Of course we will invite them but we can't expect them to be here."

"Anyone else you can think of?"

"Well, Jackie, what about Dollard? He is part of your family now, isn't he?"

"Not really. Well, I suppose he is. Well, yes. Of course he is. He is the first man Mama has really loved. And I love him too. I'll ask him."

"Jacqueline's heart has a beautiful radiance, Ian. Your future daughter-in-law is a treasure." Mac had spent the afternoon in the park with Jacqueline and Nicholas and was telling his son what he had seen. "She shows a very large love aspect. And her light is very steady."

"Eva and I don't see energy fields as clearly as you do, Dad, but we do know how our hearts respond vibrantly when Jacqueline is with us."

"She and Nick have a special resonance," Mac said. "They are like two lasers magnified by a quartz crystal. Their resonance is brilliant. It's vivid. I believe they will play a special role in the world, this couple."

"Our grandson is very lucky, Carlos, marrying a French girl. French girls are the most beautiful, n'est pas?"

156

"Of course they are, my dear Martine. Of course they are." Carlos raised his hands in surrender to his wife, a performance for the relatives who had gathered on the night before the wedding.

"And what about you, Dollard?" Monique demanded with a smile. "You agree, don't you - French girls are the most beautiful?" Dollard replied by putting his arm across her shoulders, giving her a hug, and kissing her on the forehead.

"Ian?" Eva raised an eyebrow toward her husband.

"Good grief, gentlemen," Ian said, looking around the circle in mock dismay. "How did we all get so lucky?" Eva kissed him.

"And what about you, Monsieur?" Monique leaned over to put her hand on Mac's arm. "What is your opinion?"

Mac assumed the diplomatic stance of his foreign service colleagues, drew himself up in an exaggerated, quietly dignified manner and announced, "My opinion is that all women are beautiful, especially French women, my granddaughter Gwynneth, who is half French, my daughter Lisa, and my sister Patricia and her daughter."

On another dimension, Aiya and Ohruu merged in an enhanced resonance, refining their concordance, amplifying their common band of vibration, and expanding the sound of their intention. They were turning their resonance up another notch so the personalities of their two human instruments, on the eve of their wedding day, would become similarly resonant. Their intention was the imperative of souls - the expression of Oneness.

In accordance with rules for souls, their impulses of intention were only as strong as their form personalities could handle; otherwise, there could be a breakdown in their contact with their instruments. Thus, their personalities did not always hear the intention signal clearly – only when the instrument had been refined sufficiently was soul's message heard clearly. Until then, the instrument played an approximation of soul's note, with a fidelity that reflected the degree of refinement of the instrument.

In most cases, souls could not make a strong statement until their personalities had reached the maturity of a twenty-eight or twenty-nine year old. However, both Jacqueline and Nicholas, who were twenty-five years old, were already mature enough, because of the hold on the form world their souls had developed in earlier incarnations, to carry an unusually clear expression of soul's intention.

"Ladies and gentlemen, Mesdames et Messieurs. Friends." The tall Frenchman spoke to the assembly of family members who were seated before a cloud of roses growing over an arbor in the garden of the country home where Mac had retired. He was Alain L'Heureux, a graduate student who had taught one of the courses Jacqueline had taken at the university in Paris. "There is a special something about Alain," Jacqueline had said. "He seems to know something more than the other lecturers, something profound, yet present – something coming from deep in his heart." Alain was not surprised when the couple asked him to come to London to conduct their wedding ceremony and he immediately agreed.

"In a few moments," Alain said, speaking English without a trace of accent, "we will share in marking another milestone in a journey of love which obviously began long ago." From a seat at the back of the gathering, Mac connected esoterically with Alain and enhanced the purity of light Alain radiated. He knew Alain as a senior disciple who had come to earth on a specific mission with others in his esoteric group. Their combined light embraced the audience.

"Before Jacqueline and Nicholas arrive here with us in this beautiful setting," Alain continued, "would you all be kind enough to take two minutes for silent reflection on our purpose here today, our purpose being to consecrate, in the human form, the soul's mission of Oneness."

In the silence, Ohruu and Aiya stepped up their vibration another notch, their work supported by the refined expression of Mac and Alain. The vibration touched all hearts and opened them in an expansiveness which was contagious – all in the group joining as One.

The two minutes of silence ended when, from behind the arbor, a joyful excerpt from a Chopin piano concerto rose from a small organ and animated the open hearts. As the music played, Nicholas emerged from the guest cottage with Lloyd at his side. As they walked toward the arbor, Nicholas flicked the back of his hand at Lloyd's arm. "It's Lisa, Lloyd. It's Aunt Lisa playing the organ." Lloyd just smiled, pleased that he had kept the secret. Nicholas detoured to give his aunt a hug and a kiss as she continued to play, then rejoined Lloyd in front of the arbor.

As the organ segued to a movement from a harpsichord suite by Handel, Jacqueline stepped from the conservatory with Carole and Gwynneth just behind her. They walked slowly toward the arbor, approaching from behind the gathered guests. The three were dressed simply in afternoon wear – Jacqueline in a quiet pastel blue, with no hat and no jewelry. She carried a single red rose from Nicholas, which Lloyd had delivered to her that morning.

When Jacqueline reached the arbor, Alain asked the couple to face one another and hold hands. As they did so their lights joined in a brighter radiance. "Jacqueline Louise Garneau and Nicholas Lawrence Cameron, by coming together in the way you have, you show you have responded to souls' intention for you. Your boundless love for one another, which is obvious to all of us, is a beautiful expression of soul's magnetically attractive force. More than that, you bring your love to our human condition as a healing quality. It is a gift which will only grow deeper as your life together unfolds in its all-encompassing beauty."

On their own dimension, Aiya and Ohruu continued to take advantage of the facilitating context of light to enhance even more the brightness of their co-existence.

"It matters not," Alain continued, "which of your national heritages you may claim – French or English or Chilean or Scottish – the reality is, as a soul-impressed unit, your citizenship is humanity, your home is Life. That is *the* message of our times, the message of this millennium. And that is the message, Jacqueline and Nicholas, which your Oneness manifests. Your Oneness is the magic of the Christ Impulse."

Alain gestured to the couple, smiling. "Please," he said. Jacqueline rose up on her toes and put her arms around Nicholas' shoulders. Nicholas bent down and held her around the waist. They closed their eyes and kissed gently, serenely. Alain, Lloyd, Carole and Gwynneth then stood to one side as the couple faced the guests to speak the words which would give public form to their inner act of coming together as One. Side by side, they linked arms and held hands, then spoke as a single voice: "In the name of Unity, in the Light of Soul, we pledge our lives in service of humanity and the Christ Impulse."

An upswell of livance accompanied their words and surrounded the assembly. In the sacred silence that followed, a beautiful soprano voice started to sing a love song which only a few of those gathered had heard before. The words were clear, the melody pure: "Our love becomes our life, to live in harmony and peace . . ."

"That's one of Grandpa Mac's poems," Nicholas whispered to Jacqueline. "But who wrote the music? And who is singing?" He looked questioningly at Lloyd but Lloyd refused to meet his eye.

"Nick, look." Jacqueline nudged him to look toward the back of the garden. There, walking toward them as she sang, was his Great Aunt Patricia.

". . .Our light unto the world, its pain and suffering to ease . . ."

Their honeymoon stopover in Paris was brief – only long enough for a reception for a dozen of Jacqueline's friends. Then it was off to the Italian Alps and a tiny village above Aosta. Their room in the pension looked out at snow-covered peaks which fed the tumbling river in the valley below. In these surroundings, they would explore the vistas of their future together as they enjoyed the vistas of their daily hikes in the mountains.

"It is so beautiful, Nick. Look at all the wild flowers." They paused to rest on a log beside a small rivulet splashing down a rocky channel. "Everything has its own beauty – the colors, the movement, the shapes, the expansiveness of it all. I see why you love the mountains." The experience of nature was new to Jacqueline, her life having been centered in Paris. Nicholas, on the other hand, had spent many happy days tramping through the English countryside and the Scottish highlands, and several weeks skiing and hiking in the Alps.

"My Grandpa Mac brought me to these mountains – three summers we were here, ten or twelve years ago. We hiked and talked and I asked questions and he answered with more questions. He helped me learn so much about myself, about nature, and about the world. About life, really."

"You are very close to your grandfather, Nick. Tell me about him."

"Ever since I can remember, he has been there for me as a loving presence and as a wonderful guiding friend. You've spent some hours with him, Jackie. What do you think of him?"

"He is so reserved, yet seems so wise, so knowing about life. And he is so kind."

"When I was away at sea, I communicated regularly with many friends, giving them the tourist report. But when I communicated with Grandpa Mac, I discussed what I was learning from the ship's engineer. You know, about the physics of light and sound and what physicists are telling us about soul. Grandpa explained to me how he related all those ideas to the way he sees energy fields and to his highly sensitive intuition. He was also a kind of super tutor for both Lloyd and me all during our university studies. He is a very special human being."

"Nick, when he and I spoke in the garden on our wedding day, he said he would be passing on very soon, but he would always be near us."

"Did he say that to you? That was a very private statement."

"I know. He is such a private man."

"My father says Grandpa has to keep his privacy because he works in a special way with energy fields in a macro way – whatever that is. To do that, Dad says, he needs to minimize his contact with the energy static of humanity's mental chatter and emotional turbulence - what Dad calls 'esoteric noise'."

"He does have some contact with people though. I mean, he's not a hermit."

"No, not at all. He lives quite normally, although quietly. Also, he apparently teaches a small group about energies. Dad says Grandpa's intuition tells him who is ready to hear about the deep knowing he has. He only speaks about these things to people with willing ears."

162

"Maybe he'll show us the way on our Path, and tell us where we can be of greatest service."

"Maybe he will – he certainly knows we have willing ears."

Aiya and Ohruu followed the conversation with interest. "We'll see how much Grandpa Mac leads these two," Ohruu mused. "Grandpa Mac is a very wise man and knows he cannot interfere in their search, for it is in the search that the learning is most productive – the unending search."

"And usually, Ohruu, the more difficult the search, the greater the learning."

"Yes. My Jacqueline is a case in point. When she was a small child, her Mama and Grandmaman gave her love and security but their relationships with men were singularly unsuccessful examples for her. Her Mama has only now, with Dollard, come to a true relationship of love. So Jacqueline has had to do her own search for understanding about relationships. She has had to call on all the mastery of persona I have developed over my many incarnations and bring it to the surface. That's how she found her way to Nicholas, to know he was the one."

"We'll see now what they will do with their combined learning."

The two newlyweds held hands as they scanned the mountain scenery while silently scanning the horizons of their minds, thinking about how their future might unfold, what their willing ears might hear and their open eyes might see. "You don't see much of your parents, Nick," Jackie observed. "They seem to have very busy lives."

"Yes, they're busy – and don't forget I haven't lived at home for several years."

"When you are at home, do they talk to you about their work, or do they keep it to themselves?"

FREEING THE LIGHT OF SOUL

"They talk about it all the time. They have an intense urge to bring their work out into the world."

"Just what is their work? I know it isn't their day jobs."

"They gather with friends in the evening and on weekends and work with energies. They say they are bringing a new stream of life into manifestation through very specific training in energy sensitivity. Their purpose, they say, is to join esoterically with many other groups in the world that have a similar intent, and use that energy stream in a way that makes peace our norm, a natural way of living. Although I have sometimes joined them in their groups, I'm not exactly sure how that works. They say their work is common now all over the world."

"How long have they been doing that work?"

"They started their energy work, according to Grandpa Mac, in 2005, just before I was born. One day in the city my Dad was struck - in Grandpa's words - 'by an electrical shock of insight'. Grandpa said that Mother, in a way, caught it immediately from Dad. He says similar bolts of enlightenment struck a thousand or more people all over the world at about the same time. He says it was the Reappearance of the Christ principle, manifest in many – the One Thousand Awakenings to the Love Impulse. My parents also spend many hours working for an organization that supports education and health care in Africa. They say it is a way of continuing their love affair with the African people."

"What a wonderful atmosphere for you to grow up in. That's why it is so natural for you to work with esoteric ideas." Jacqueline closed her eyes to absorb more fully what her husband had just said about the awakenings to the Love Impulse. They had discussed theories about the technology of the Love Impulse in Alain's seminars. She remembered reading reports of some of the unusual happenings early in the century, only later seeing them as a single esoteric action. She wondered what Alain knew about the One Thousand Awakenings. *He wouldn't know first hand, of course - he was only eight years old in 2005 and the reports were all about adults. And what about Nicholas and I? Are we alive to the Love Impulse,* she wondered. *We definitely aligned with something special during our wedding ceremony.*

She squeezed her husband's hand and asked, "Do you think we are alive to the Love Impulse, Nick? Have we been awakened like the One Thousand?"

"I don't know, sweetheart. I think we try to be as loving as we can, but I don't think we are among the Awakened – not yet. Grandpa Mac did say our life work will be to serve the Love Impulse."

"That must mean we will work for peace too. Like your parents. Isn't that what it means to serve the Love Impulse, Nick? To work for peace in the world?"

"I think that's what it means, my darling. Anyway, it can't hurt if we work for peace." He pulled her close to him and kissed her, his heart swelling in their expanding love.

She interrupted the kiss and whispered, "So, Nicholas my husband, that will be our life."

"Our life, Jacqueline, my wife," he whispered back, kissing her again.

Later, as they sat on their hotel room balcony with tea and sweets, Jackie's declaration – 'that will be our life' – came back to Nicholas for further thought. It was easy to say and easy to agree, but what does it mean, he wondered. She will probably come up with some practical ideas while his mind wanders into many possibilities. His wife's thinking ran deep - deep, thorough and wise was she. He remembered being impressed by the depth of her intelligence when they had tea that rainy day in London so many moons ago.

Jackie squeezed his arm as they sat in silence, eyes closed, letting the warm summer sun soak into their bodies. Then, "I've been thinking, Nick."

"Thinking about what, Love?"

"About how everything fits together."

"Fits together, Love? What do you mean?"

"I mean, what you have learned in reading and writing on philosophy and religion, and all you learned from Grandpa Mac and your ship's engineer and your parents. And what I have learned in my studies of esoteric psychology and my esoteric healing seminars with Alain."

"Okay, Love. So how does it fit?"

"They go together, Nick - my esoteric healing and your energy studies and writing. We can teach people to see their lives as energy and what that means for how they handle their everyday lives."

"Hmm. Why not? Your learning about human energies; my learning about the ocean of energies in which we dwell. It does sort of fit, Love."

"And all energies are the One Life."

"That's one of Grandpa Mac's themes."

"You know, Nick, most people these days are conscious of human energy fields. In the last fifty years, there has been so much development of energy therapies and so much research on the mind-body connection - the awareness is widespread. People are ready now for more depth, and we can learn how to bring that. You and I could learn more about the science of human and global energy fields, and organize teaching modules to make it everyday practical and accessible to everyone."

"When people know as a fact, not just an idea, that they are truly One Life, surely peace will prevail on earth."

"If we can do that, Jackie, our wedding pledge for peace will be fulfilled."

"Then it is our imperative, isn't it Nicholas dear?"

"It must be, my love."

"I can't wait to get started – to teach what we are learning."

"You are wonderful, my Jacqueline." He kissed her hand, then her cheek, then her lips.

They sat quietly, watching the sun ease lower toward the mountains, letting their thoughts sort themselves out, letting their youthful idealism solidify, letting their commitment sink in.

Jacqueline squeezed Nick's arm, a prelude to her next proposal. "And Nicholas, we could make that learning a part of everyone's normal basic education for life – at home and in school, not just in special courses, or on one day a week."

He kissed her again. "That's the way it should be, Love." He snuggled his bride closer to him as they both lifted their eyes to take in the grandeur of their surroundings.

"These mountains are such a wonderful inspiration, Nick."

Aiya and Ohruu appreciated the couple's response to the higher frequency Love Impulse the two souls had animated in the Nicholas and Jacqueline personalities. At their young age, their conscious awareness of soul's action was faint, but their minds were open and their hearts were strong. Now the mountains were again doing their magic, creating ideal conditions for the two souls to raise their presence in their two personalities. In another three or four years, Nicholas and Jacqueline would begin consciously to register their souls' presence.

Chapter Twenty-Five

The Early Years: Preparation

"Jackie!" Nicholas called to his wife as soon as he came through the door of their flat. "Jackie, are you ready to move to Johannesburg, Love?"

"Johannesburg? Of course. Or Hamburg or Gothenburg or Pittsburgh. Any Burg you want. Now will you please go back out the door, mon amour. Then come in again, take your coat off, give me a kiss, and tell me about your day."

"Jackie, it's happened," he persisted. "The network has asked me to be chief correspondent and head of the news bureau in South Africa. It's a promotion. And it's Africa, Jackie."

"Oh Nick. That's wonderful. After just three years, and you're only twenty-eight, Nick. They must really like your work."

"They said they like my political reporting. My boss said it has depth and that's what they want coming out of Africa."

"Oh, Nicholas, you've dreamed of going to Africa ever since you were a small boy, haven't you." She put her arms around his neck, seeing some of the small boy still shining through.

"Mom and Dad talked about it all the time. They met in an African village, remember, when they were working there. And Grandpa Mac has shown me hundreds of photographs my great grandfather took when he traveled all over the continent. It's true,

Jackie. It has been a dream – one I've always believed would come true."

"So you'll accept the offer?" She stepped back to look into his eyes.

"I don't know." He hugged her, then turned to take off his coat. "In one way I really want to go. Not just because it's Africa. This is a really good job – in charge of the bureau, Jackie. I could really do something. On the other hand, I know you are happy in your counseling job and we have only been married three years. I hate to scramble things at this stage."

"We can make it work."

"Do you think?"

"Whatever you decide, dear, I'll be with you."

"I know you will, Love."

"Why don't you talk to Lloyd? He has a probing mind. He'll help you think it through."

"Take it, Man. You may never get another chance." Lloyd's enthusiasm was not what Nicholas expected. Lloyd worked nine to five in a physics laboratory and wasn't given to adventure. Was he projecting a hidden desire? "You've always wanted to go to Africa, Nick, and now you're getting it on a platter."

"I don't think it's fair to Jackie, Lloyd."

"Well, that's for the two of you to decide. Think about it, though. Last week when you were at our place for dinner, you both said you were itching to do something different, something more significant. Doreen told me afterward she wouldn't be surprised if both of you were to change jobs pretty soon."

"Your wife is very sensitive to people's thoughts."

"Well, it was obvious even to me the two of you were unsettled about something."

"But is Johannesburg something more significant? Or is it just more of the same in a different location?"

169

"Don't underestimate the significance of what the two of you are doing, my friend. A free society depends on people like you telling us how it is in the world. As for Jackie, her counseling therapy has helped hundreds of people. You are both doing good stuff."

"I suppose we are, Lloyd. Nevertheless, it may not be enough. There is something important stirring inside. Something is moving me and I don't know what it is. It's the same for Jackie."

"Make the break, then. Just do it. Go to Africa and see what happens. Have some fun while you're at it. You need it. You deserve it."

"We've barely gotten established here."

"So it should be easy to leave. We'll come and visit you – we'll all go on safari."

"It does sound exciting. And it is a great job."

"Then go for give it, Man. Give it a try. See your dream out."

"We'll meditate on it."

As Jacqueline emerged from the bedroom, ready for the party, Nicholas stepped back to admire her in her new dress and perky hairstyle. "Wow! Thirty years old and still the most beautiful woman in all of London." Then he embraced her, careful not to disturb the perfect picture, and kissed her.

"Merci, mon amour. You're looking pretty cool yourself. I like your new haircut."

He kissed her again. "Happy thirtieth birthday, Love."

"Happy thirtieth birthday to you too."

"By the way, Love, how come you decided we should give ourselves a birthday party? Aren't our friends supposed to do that for us? What happened to tradition?"

"This is tradition – a very old one. The bad spirits are most mischievous on birthdays, you know. So, we're gathering friends to scare all the bad spirits away, and we'll light candles to send prayers up to the gods."

"Oh, good. We'll need all that help in our new life."

"I'm sure the gods will be with us, Nick."

"Wait till we tell everyone what we're doing. I wonder what Lloyd and Doreen will say."

"I'm glad you didn't take the Johannesburg job, Nick. If you had, we wouldn't be making these plans."

"I'm glad too, dear. We don't know, though, Jackie, what Africa might have led to. Lloyd nearly had me convinced it would be a great springboard. He was very persuasive. It was quite funny, coming from such a cautious, steady guy."

"Easy to throw someone else's caution to the wind, I guess."

"People are going to start arriving soon. Are you ready, dear?" The doorbell rang.

"I guess I am. They're here." She opened the door and their two best friends came noisily into the flat.

"Happy Birthday, Jackie. Happy Birthday, Nick." Lloyd and Doreen gave them both hugs and kisses. "Here. Open these. We've brought you the latest magical way to keep your lives in order."

"A picture calendar. Thank you." Jackie unfolded the pages. "With pictures of London. They are absolutely beautiful. You took these photos, Lloyd?"

"Yes, I did. Doree and I were sure you would soon be on the move – somewhere - so we wanted you to remember where your friends are."

"Well, wait till we tell you."

"See, Doree, we were right. They are on the move."

The doorbell rang again and more people arrived. Neighbors and friends from the network, from Jackie's counseling center, and from Nick's Cambridge days crowded into their modest flat. Nick and Jackie welcomed them each with a hug and introduced them to the other guests. In the dining room, the buffet brimmed with attractive organic vegetarian dishes; a colorful bowl of carbonated fruit punch sat on a side table surrounded by glass cups; a large three-tiered cake with white and blue icing was the centerpiece of the dining room table. Two blue candles, in the shape of the number thirty, nestled on the top of the cake.

When everyone had arrived, Lloyd rattled a spoon on a glass to get the crowd's attention. "Quiet please. Our hosts have an announcement."

"Yes, we do," Nicholas began. "This is a rather important birthday for us. Today, both of us gave our employers notice that we are leaving." They got the surprised exclamations they expected. "In thirty days," Nick continued over the noise, "Jackie and I will both be out of a job." Now there were puzzled expressions.

"Out of our current jobs," Jackie assured them, "but starting new jobs."

"Jackie will join the human energy research project which our friend Alain L'Heureux is leading, and I will take a leap into freelance writing. We'll both continue working out of London."

"Well, congratulations." Lloyd led the line of hugs for the two. "At least you are not moving away – yet."

"We've known for ages that something was in the wind." Doreen gave them an extra long hug. "Didn't Alain ask you to join the project two years ago, Jackie? How come it took all this time to decide?"

"Oh, you know me, Doreen. I have to let things simmer for a long time. We also had to work out how I would operate from London while the research is centered in Paris."

"Jackie takes her time, you know, to think things through and get it right." Nick put his arm around his wife's shoulder and squeezed her closer to him. "But once you decide, Love, you are there two hundred percent."

"On the other hand, you, my dear, were ready to go to Johannesburg in a second. You saw freedom and challenge beckoning - your two pillars of life."

"And now freelancing." Lloyd shook his head and frowned. "I guess that's real freedom for you, Nick - freedom from security. How are you going to make a living?"

The cautious Lloyd showing up, Nick thought. "I have some ideas, old man," he assured his close friend. "Maybe an internet magazine column. Maybe a serialized book on the internet. Some thought-piece broadcast documentaries. No end to the possibilities. I'll be a free lance – an independent roving knight, available for hire."

"Nicholas will be very successful," Jackie affirmed. "You wait and see."

"It has been seven years since you left your network job for freelancing, Nick. I admit I was a skeptic then. But now, things are really coming together for you. Everyone is talking about your latest piece on the new world religion." Lloyd showed him a printout of his study group's analysis. "Our group was unanimous. We all said your insight untangled a lot of knots."

"It did seem to touch a hot wire in a lot of people, didn't it?"

"Hot wire, indeed," chimed Doreen as she arrived on the terrace with a pot of tea and biscuits. The four friends were spending the weekend together in a country cottage they often rented in the Cotswold Hills. "Your ideas blew fuses in some traditional circles, Nick. Not that those circuits carry much power these days."

"Maybe not, Doree dear," her husband cautioned, "but their voices get pretty loud when it comes to the radical new religion Nick talks about."

"Radical?" Jackie raised her eyebrows. "Nick merely established the relationship between humans and God in energy terms. That's not radical any more." Jackie's Gallic shrug said as much as her words. "They are even using Nick's writing in some of the high schools in America."

"Maybe not radical to everyone, Jackie, but a buzzer nevertheless for the establishment. It was Nick's way of expressing it that raised their alarm bells, wasn't it Doree?" Lloyd turned to his wife for support.

"Perfect crystal clarity," Doreen agreed.

"Yes, clarity. Sharp clarity. It penetrated our thick minds and let the fresh air circulate." Lloyd had been noticing how his own very scientific mind was loosening up and opening to new ways of learning. "Simple words, simple ideas, profound effect."

"Your audience is growing with every piece you produce, Nicholas. Look." Doreen showed him a current news bulletin from an international publication. "Your work turns up everywhere."

"He's becoming world famous." Jacqueline's pride in her husband was obvious.

"World famous? Well, maybe somewhat well known in the English language," Nicholas acknowledged.

"Nick says the words are just coming to him more easily now," Jackie explained. "He's reaching into the intuitive plane of pure reason and he's getting better every day, aren't you dear."

"It's a matter of tuning, if you know what I mean," Nick tried to explain. How could he put into words his easy access to wisdom?

"I think I know what you mean." Doreen also had a finely tuned sensitivity. "The clear thoughts are there, aren't they; we only have to find their frequency to let them through."

"Jackie does the same in her energy work," Nick pointed out. "Her work with health and healing starts with her intuition."

"Yes, I do work intuitively more and more. It seems to be more available these past three or four years. Intuition gives more certainty in diagnosis and more precision in bringing the correct energy modalities to the patient's needs."

"Your research with Alain is complete, then?"

"Not really, Doreen. Alain is expanding his research but my emphasis has shifted to clinical applications of our research, and I am beginning to train other health workers and healers. I'll continue with a part of the research, though, alongside the teaching and clinical work."

"It sounds as though you have entered quite a new phase, Jackie." Lloyd had noticed her voice took on a different tone when she spoke about training healers. "Are your own energies changing?"

"Another phase in the cycle? Maybe so. I think it started a year or two ago. We humans often work in seven year cycles. Maybe age thirty-five was a turning point for me."

"And you, Nick? You've done philosophy, religion, ethics, social conscience. You've organized gatherings of people of diverse beliefs and helped them find common ground. You've done broadcasts, articles, a book, a documentary. And your speeches - people now think of you as a leading peace activist. What's next? Or has it already started?"

"You do have ideas about something new, don't you Nick." Doreen could read the themes in some people's minds. "I can tell you have some well-formulated thoughts."

"Well, Nick?" Lloyd spread his arms, waiting for Nick's answer. "What's next, my friend?"

Chapter Twenty-Six

The Middle Years: Thy Will Be Done

"Can you believe we're actually here, Nick? In the Rocky Mountains? It's another world."

"A long way from the dust and heat we've endured for the past year." Nicholas and Jacqueline were deeply fatigued and more than ready for their two-week retreat in the mountains. They had just spent six uninterrupted months of long and challenging days working in a dozen locations across India and Pakistan. Before that, they had been six months in the Middle East, six months in China, three months in Northern Ireland and three months in the Balkans.

"We really need this break, Nick. We've been at it too hard for too long."

"Have we ever. You know, Love, we wouldn't have survived but for our ability to stay centered and aligned with our purpose."

"Our inner peace lets us deal more easily with the outer turmoil."

"Still, my bones have been creaking under the weight of all of my forty-two years."

"I'm glad we decided to come here."

"You can actually feel the mountains rejuvenating our poor old bodies, can't you Jackie." Nicholas took a deep breath as though cleansing his mind as well as his lungs. "Climbing up this mountain is like climbing out of a fog."

"We've been climbing for an hour, Nick. Let's stop for a rest and enjoy the view." They slipped from the straps of their daypacks, settled themselves on a patch of heather among the boulders nature had strewn down the slope, and stretched out on their backs.

"Look at the color of that lake down there, Nick. Isn't it beautiful? So green. Emerald green."

"It's the glacial silt suspended in the water that refracts the light and makes it look green."

"We'll have to thank the ambassador for recommending the lodge to us."

"We were lucky to get reservations, just dropping in like we did." They had made a snap decision about where to spend their break and caught a flight to the airport in the city at the edge of the foothills. They had called the mountain lodge just that morning to get a room. The transfer into the mountains was swift and the lodge hostess welcomed them warmly. Within an hour, they were hiking up a rough trail on a steep slope where avalanches had cleared away the forest, leaving scrub trees and low bushes and loose debris from above.

Jackie shifted so she could rest her head on Nick's shoulder. "Timeless mountains," she sighed, "we surrender." She closed her eyes and turned her face toward the afternoon sun to catch as much as she could of its healing rays.

"Thy will be done," said Nick, joining her surrender. It had been a long three years, and now their travels were over.

"You've been where?" Nick and Jackie were having breakfast on the lodge verandah with a couple who had arrived at the lodge the day before for a weekend of hiking. The questioner was a geologist who had worked in several overseas countries. When Nick mentioned they had been in the Middle East, the man stopped his coffee cup half way to his lips. "I've worked in the region for several years. May I ask what you were doing there?"

"I'm a journalist, Byron, and Jackie teaches human energy healing."

"Human energy healing? Interesting." Byron's wife, Hazel, was a trainer at a community recreation center and knew about the energies of the subtle bodies.

"What exactly were you doing?" Byron asked

"I've been gathering material," Nick continued, "for a comprehensive documentary about our spiritual instincts and the world's major religions. I believe it will show dramatically, scientifically and conclusively the fact of the fundamental oneness of all life. It will show how humans distort that fact and create the divisions which have been the source of so many problems in the world. It will also show, I hope, how we can heal those divisions. I call the project, Our One Life."

"Wow. Is that all?" The man put his hand to his brow. "Whew! Did you hear that, Hazel?" His wife absorbed Nick's story without comment.

"And wherever we went, Jackie organized programs to teach local health workers some paradigm-breaking modalities for energy healing that she and a French researcher have developed. She does very special work."

"In a way," Jackie added, "we are both working at healing."

"How did all this get started? Did somebody hire you?"

"Nobody hired us, Byron, but we do have funding from a British foundation - we're British, in case you hadn't noticed our accent. I was a freelance journalist for eight years, writing for several publishing and broadcast outlets, digging into whatever subjects caught my eye. In the latter two or three years I found I was deep into those fundamental questions about the meaning of life. I decided to tackle the topic whole – hit a home run, as you might say over here. In that same period, Jackie had started something new in her work."

"What was that, Jackie?" asked Hazel.

"So many people wanted to learn about our new health and healing modalities that my research and clinical work evolved into a teaching program. I developed teaching modules that were very successful and decided I should share them. I did that wherever we went so the application of our research has spread rapidly."

"What is your approach?"

"We have three applications: prevention, self-healing, and intimate contact with soul."

"Are there people doing your kind of healing in America?"

"Oh yes, Hazel. Several. Some were part of the original research group. Some worked with me during the year we were here before our overseas travels."

"You worked in America too?"

As Nick recalled the year in America, it seemed like ages ago. "We were in the U.S. for about a year at the beginning, making preparations for our travels. We spent time with academics, natural healers, scientists, theologians, diplomats, people at the UN, immigrants from the regions we were going to visit - anyone who could give us background information about our topic and the different cultures and religious beliefs. We also assembled our production crews – different crews for different regions. And of course we had to arrange for visas, living accommodations, transportation and so on."

Byron looked at his watch. "Hazel Honey, friends, I hate to break up this discussion, but it's late – almost nine o'clock. The morning is half gone."

Hazel checked her own watch, calculating their hiking time. "Byron, if we . . . " she started.

"Come on, Hazel." Byron started to push his chair away from the table. "We've got to hit the trail if we're going to get back before dark."

"What a pity." Hazel didn't hide her disappointment. "But I'm afraid Byron is right. "Will you keep on traveling to teach, Jackie?"

"I really don't know. Maybe."

"And your documentary, Nick – is it finished now?"

"It will take another year or so, Byron, to complete the editing and bring out the finished productions. We have a global message and we will deliver it in several languages and use several different formats suited to different media and cultures. We assembled a great production team before we started traveling. It is an enlivened group and they know what we are trying to do. They have things well in hand, so I'll just check in with them periodically. My part of it is virtually finished."

"Then what, Nick?" Byron asked. "Do you have another documentary lined up?"

"We've been so focused for so long on getting our work done each day, we haven't had time to think about anything else. We both need time to catch our breath. That's why we have come here."

Jackie stretched her arms out to take in the natural surroundings. "Today we are enjoying the beauty of this day and these mountains. Tomorrow? Who knows what tomorrow will bring?"

They all stood and shook hands. "It was a pleasure to meet you."

"When you arrived at the lodge, I couldn't help noticing from your baggage tags that you've just come from India," the young porter said. Nick and Jackie were standing on the lodge porch after dinner, breathing in the evening light on the lake. They had spent a leisurely day walking a trail through the forests nearby, stopping frequently to admire the mountains, the patterns in the trees, the busyness of the birds and squirrels. "My grandparents are from India," the young man explained, "and I plan to visit their home after I finish university."

"Do you still have relatives there, Herb?" Jackie asked, reading his name from the pin he wore.

"So I'm told, but I've never met any of them."

"Tell me, Herb, what do you know about the trails around here?" Nick was looking now at a large tabletop model of the mountains and lakes around the lodge. "We're trying to decide on a hiking route for tomorrow."

"I've been on every trail in the area. What kind of hike are you looking for?"

"Somewhere away from the busy trails."

"Yes, somewhere quiet – where we can sit and contemplate the world." As she spoke, Jackie took hold of Nick's upper arm with both her hands and put her head against his chest.

"Then, I suggest the Glacier Trail." Herb pointed to a white patch on the model which represented a glacier nestled along the side of a mountain, then with his finger traced a route from the lodge to a small lake at the margin of the glacier. "On the way, you'll cover three or four distinct kinds of terrain. Along the lakeside here, and then across an alluvial fan, you are on level ground. Then you climb up a rocky slope – it's pretty steep with a lot of switchbacks – then it continues up across open stretches of shale before it levels out through the trees over the pass. Then this last stretch of trail, you see, is across bedrock and lateral moraines to the edges of the glacier. Along here, the trail faces south, so you'll have the full sun there."

He showed them good places to stop for lunch and for their time of contemplation. "Not many people go up there because the trail isn't well marked. But I can give you exact directions and you won't have any trouble." His smile widened. "And the view is glorious all the way."

"Herb was right, Nick. These switchbacks are steep."

"We're making good time, Love. Let's stop for a snack." They were at an opening in the forest and found a comfortable place to sit with a full view of the valley below.

"Look where we've come from, Nick. You can see the trail all the way back to the lodge."

"I've been thinking about where we've come from, Jackie – I mean, where we've come from these last four years." He gave her a hug. "You know, I think we've done good work."

Jackie put her hands around his arm. "I think we have, mon amour." This retreat was a time to gather up and integrate their experiences, and bring closure to another chapter of their lives.

Nick looked at his project as a capstone on all his work on religion and philosophy. He had plunged into the project with a driving intensity of purpose. It was his attempt to blast away at the foundations of religious, racial and tribal conflict. He wanted to reveal and celebrate the common and inspiring truths which were at the source of all the major world religions, and were the teachings of the Ancient Wisdom. This would help clear the space, he hoped, for people to see the light of the Love Impulse more clearly, and for the forces striving toward a New World to seize humanity's evolution more firmly.

He had built his production around the profound revelations he had absorbed from the broad reach of intelligence he was learning to touch with his higher mind. He had discovered the scope of his mind's intelligence during their preparation year when he was reaching to a higher frequency of soul vibration for inspiration about his project. He was now able to tune to the ideals flowing from, what he called, the essence of the evolutionary will that propelled humanity forward. He translated those ideals as a paradigm for change in how we think and live, in order to bring peace and harmony to the world.

He framed the production with a comprehensive and scholarly body of scientific, theological and racial research, and the determined personal beliefs of scores of clerics and laypersons, politicians and peacemakers. A panel of intuitive sensitives cooperated with him to bring it all together in a beautifully intelligent synthesis. His broadcast peers would later treat his work as a hallmark of journalistic innovation. The world's thinkers were still pouring over his prescriptions for peace.

The project had grown out of the seed of an idea, which he and Lloyd Williams had formulated at Cambridge and Nick had nourished for twenty years. He had given it preliminary shape as he worked on his earlier documentaries. When the concept finally matured in his mind, the resources simultaneously appeared. The Sir James Cameron Foundation provided financial backing for the project – no surprise there - and the World for People Network helped him with technical and logistics support.

While Nick drove his project, Jackie engaged local energy healers and other health care professionals in a program of experiential learning that opened their eyes and, more importantly, their hearts, to new healing possibilities. She had become skilled in introducing people easily and naturally to her healing modalities. She started from their own healing traditions and led them into the most advanced esoteric healing structures, using her sensitivity to the energies of the subtle bodies and the play of the seven rays in each individual. She combined these structures with the latest scientific research on human energy systems and her own intuitive sight. She helped them to see the subjective realities of soul and the human condition, and the implications for new ways of healthy living, new ways of diagnosing disease, and new, more effective techniques of treatment. She had guided literally hundreds of health practitioners into new realms of understanding and service.

"I think our souls are singing, Jackie. I think we are well aligned with soul's purpose."

"Is that why we are so content – our souls are content with their work?"

"Do you remember the discontent of our late twenties when we quit our jobs because we wanted to do something more significant?"

"Yes, I remember it well, Nick dear."

"I think that was the first touch of soul's vibration that got through to our personalities. The discontent started again in our mid-thirties when we each started pushing our work further – you went from research, to clinical practice, to teaching; I went from a discussion format, to stating new propositions, to creating the One Life project."

"You're talking about the cycles of soul, aren't you - soul animating a corresponding cycle in the affairs of the personality."

"Exactly."

"We've talked before about soul's cycles, Nick – the theory of it."

"Grandpa Mac used to talk about it. He used to say we follow a cycle: we take a new initiative, it meets the resistance of the old way, there is a crisis, then resolution, and finally integration. When I think about the struggles and victories in our own life patterns, it's no longer theory. It is totally real."

"So do you think our souls are now in a quiet integration phase and that's why we're content?"

"When we feel content, it may be we haven't yet felt soul's next initiative."

"Oh, Nick. Please. We came here for a rest, not another call to action."

"We'll see. We know whatever we do is personality's expression of soul's journey toward oneness. The only question is how purely we express soul's will."

"Right. So, our work these past three or four years, Jackie – do you think we have been true to our soul's purpose?

Jackie squeezed his upper arm and nestled into his shoulder. "I don't know about soul, Nick, but if Papa Carlos is looking down on what you've done, he probably wouldn't recognize it as his old profession of journalism, but I think he would be proud of you."

"And if Nana Martine could see what you do, Jackie, she would be amazed and would wonder what had become of the healing arts and her nursing profession. And just think what Mama Monique and Dollard would say about your magic."

"You know what Dollard would say, Nick." Jackie mimicked Dollard's deep warm voice, " 'How can I help you do more of that, my dear,' and then he would reach for his check book."

"And Monique?"

"Mama would say, 'That's wonderful, Jacqueline'." Jackie mimicked Monique's voice and gestures perfectly and Nick burst out laughing. She reminded him of how much he had loved Monique's strength and enthusiasm. "Then she would say, 'Now, Jacqueline, what are you going to do next?'."

"I do miss them, Jackie. They passed over too soon for my liking."

"I miss them too, Nick. But let's not even think about what we are going to do next."

"It is so good to see you home again, you two." Doreen poured some tea. "Here, have some of my shortbread. Lloyd and I have really missed you, you know."

"Thank you, Doreen. Well, you can't imagine how happy we are to see the two of you again." Jackie sipped her tea. "This tea tastes so good – it always tastes better at home. There have been so many times in so many places I wished we could sit down for tea with you and Lloyd."

"We've hardly seen you for - how long?" Lloyd cast his memory back. "It must be four years. An hour here, a half-hour there. Probably no more than five times in those four years."

"Probably." Nick tried to remember. "Just the few times we passed through London on our way somewhere."

"But London will be our home base for the foreseeable future." Jackie smiled at her husband. "Won't it dear. We've had enough of the gypsy life."

"So, come on, tell us all about it," Lloyd encouraged them. "Your experiences – what happened? What stands out? Are you pleased with your work? Are your projects finished? Tell us."

Nicholas laughed. "So many questions, so much to tell. Where shall we begin?"

"Why not begin at the end?" Doreen suggested, reaching over to her husband as though to calm his enthusiasm. "Your two weeks in the Rocky Mountains. Tell us first about your retreat. Are the Rockies really so wonderful?"

"Everything you've heard, and more, Doreen." Jackie sipped her tea, then began talking with both her hands and voice. It was absolutely magnificent. Being there is so . . . It is hard to describe the feelings you have when you are high in those mountains, above the tree line, above any sign of civilization, above all your cares. The mountains, they hold you in an uplifting way - a kind of inspiring aura of peace."

Lloyd nodded his understanding. "I wish we could have been there. Doree and I have talked about going, haven't we dear – one of the last great wilderness areas in North America, they say."

"Is it really such a pristine corner of the earth?" asked Doreen.

"Not so much any more, even though we were in a National Park. Once you get away from the towns and the tourist facilities, however, you can find the wilderness. We did see several animals in the wild – bear, moose, elk, deer - but their natural habitat is under tremendous pressure."

"But it was the space, the air, the nature, the ... " Jackie couldn't find the words. "The Presence," she said finally. "The Infinite Presence." Lloyd and Doreen understood.

"For two weeks we turned off our communicators – doing that in itself gave us space. Nearly every day we hiked to high elevations, and sometimes we sat for hours in silence. It was heaven."

"Once we left the lodge, we seldom saw other hikers," Jackie added.

"Usually it was just the two of us – and the Presence, as Jackie calls it – in the middle of nowhere." Nick lived the vibration of the Presence as he spoke and they all resonated to the field of energy he animated.

"Just the two of us," Jackie sighed. "It really was heavenly."

"Well, the two of us and Korry," Nick reminded her.

"Of course - Korry."

"Who is Korry?" Doreen asked.

"Korry is an old man – well, he must be over sixty-five - he works for the National Park Service," Jackie explained. "He maintains the trails – carries an axe, a saw, a shovel, and he restores the trails - clearing the deadfalls, fixing washouts, and . . ."

"And talking to the birds and the animals," Nick interjected.

"It's true, you know." Jackie chuckled at the memory. "We first met him when Nick and I were hiking up through the forest. He was sitting on a log beside a squirrel, at his feet was a porcupine, and on a branch just two feet away from his head was a raven. He seemed to be having a conversation with them all. Not feeding them – just, somehow, communicating with them. It was incredible. We just stopped and stared."

"Then he turned to us and introduced us - by our names - to his friends. What a surprise that was - he knew our names."

"He knew you? How?"

"He just said he had heard we were in the area. At the time we guessed it was because he knew someone at the lodge."

"We sat with him for an hour or more, talking about the state of the world, if you can imagine – this trail worker, in the middle of nowhere. We talked about how things have changed, especially during the forty plus years since the One Thousand Awakenings. He knew all about that."

"Korry's job is maintaining trails?"

"Yes," Nick laughed. "Maintaining trails - for travelers."

"When we left him, Lloyd, our hearts were soaring." Jackie's radiant heart center lit up as she lived her words. "Our souls were singing. You could say Life spoke."

"And we heard," said Nick. "We heard."

Aiya and Ohruu attended to what their instruments were voicing to their friends. The words of Nick and Jackie came out of their mouths on the energy streams of their souls' purpose. The couple's interpretations of their souls' impulses were clear, showing that full integration of soul and personality had occurred – full integration. This was a significant marker on soul's journey. With this infusion of the personality, soul was ready to take a more active role in the life of the instrument. Freedom was in sight.

"We saw him two more times. He just happened to be working where we were hiking."

"Just happened – sure," Lloyd said. He laughed. "And squirrels just happen to eat nuts."

Doreen brought some more tea. As she poured, her energy field brightened again, as did Lloyd's, as they resonated intuitively to the fine heart vibrations emanating from their friends.

Nick sipped the tea and continued. "In that first meeting with Korry, we heard the sound of the Oneness of Life. All life. All the abstract. All matter. We saw more completely than before our place in the whole, in the totality of Life. We knew more deeply that soul was humanity's unifying fact; we knew soul as our absolute identity."

"Yes, our absolute identity," Jackie emphasized. "We began to live the reality instead of the reflection."

Nick and Jackie realized they were speaking about matters normally unspeakable. To close collaborators like Lloyd and Doreen, however, it was acceptable. These two old friends had a sensitivity well beyond the average and understood the terms of the conversation.

"It was Korry, then," Doreen suggested. "Korry enlivened something in you."

"He did," Nick acknowledged. "Or rather, we responded to the energy of his presence. We resonated on a higher chord which removed another veil from our awareness. We dissolved another constriction and became more conscious of our deepest reality."

"Soul overtaking personality," Doreen said. She had the intuitive ability to see energy fields and, to her, the signs were clear. "Your light is showing through – brightly."

"Is it the enlightenment the Buddhists speak of?" Lloyd wondered.

"We are all, literally, beings of light, Lloyd," Nick reminded him. "You know that from your early physics courses."

"Right. It was a physicist who said that matter is really light imprisoned by gravity."

"And the Ancient Wisdom says our task in life is to free light from matter – to liberate it."

"To free the light of soul," Jackie affirmed, "by refining the matter of personality."

"I think you are both near the conclusion of your soul's struggle for control," Doreen proposed.

"We were not aware our time had come," Nick explained, "although in retrospect, we could see a pattern in our work that might have given us clues."

"Who is this Korry, then?"

"We don't really know, Lloyd." Jackie shrugged.

"Certainly someone special," Doreen suggested. "What a privilege for you to have met him."

"There's more," Nick said. "Something happened during our third meeting."

Jackie picked up the story. "Yes, much more. Our final meeting with Korry was three days before the end of our stay. It only lasted about fifteen minutes. Still, we knew, as he spoke to us, we had become something totally different."

"I don't know the words he spoke," Nick admitted, "but he opened another door for us and we just walked right through."

"It was a door to another world, wasn't it Nick, or so it seemed – a door into Korry's intimate company of souls where such love as we had never before experienced enveloped us – it overwhelmed us."

"At that moment," Nick added, "we knew our lives had changed forever. It was a little frightening – not knowing what was going to be expected of us."

Jackie continued the story. "Afterward, we hiked up to a ridge on the shoulder of one of the higher mountains in the area. We had our lunch there, overlooking a vast expanse of mountain peaks. Such space, such timelessness."

Nick nodded agreement. "And it was there, in that timeless, infinite space, we became aware of jus how our lives had changed."

"Yes, we realized our lives were no longer our own. Do you understand? We were no longer – are no longer - the persons we were before we met our company of souls."

"Looking at you now," Doreen observed, "I see something very special took place."

"Everything is different now, Doreen. Totally different. Lloyd, it is something like the difference between a physicist who sees the world as atoms, and one who sees the quantum world. The change of perspective changes everything."

"I'm beginning to see your point – I think. Are we to assume, then, we are no longer able to talk to you two about mundane earthly matters? Or are your feet still on the ground?"

"Solidly grounded, my friend," Nick assured him. "Otherwise, how could we be of service to humanity?"

"There's no chance we could lose our practicality, Lloyd. Mama wouldn't let us."

Nick laughed and told them what happened as they prepared to descend to the lodge after finishing their lunch. "Jackie turned to me and said, 'It's Mama again, Nick.' You know Monique passed on two years ago, but here she was, still speaking to Jackie."

"I heard her say to me, 'Now, what are you going to do next, Jacqueline?' She was always asking me that."

"We don't actually hear Monique, you know. For Jackie, Monique symbolizes forward movement. And we did feel a definite urge to action."

"Neither of us knew what we were going to do – something about putting to use the greater capacities we were absorbing." Jackie paused. "And fulfilling the greater responsibilities that come with them."

"The next day," Nick continued, "we hiked to another high trail and had our lunch at another magnificent viewpoint. It was spectacular, wasn't it Jackie?"

"It was breathtaking."

"After lunch, as we were just sitting quietly, enjoying the view, I looked at Jackie and at the same moment she turned and looked at me. We were literally of one mind. Without any words, we each knew what we were going to do next. And we would do it together."

"We had the answer for Mama."

Chapter Twenty-Seven

Commencement 2070

The Dean of the Faculty of Human Energy Sciences stood before the Commencement audience and began to read the dual citation which would lead to the granting of two honorary Doctor of Science degrees. He had been preceded by colleagues overseeing the granting of honorary degrees to two other recipients.

On the platform with the Dean were the university President and about a hundred faculty members, wearing academic robes of purple and crimson and gold and blue and some colors even the Dean couldn't put a name to. Behind the faculty sat the orchestra, about thirty strong, with a lot of brass shining in the bright lights. The state Governor sat to the side of the faculty with the Chair of the Board of Trustees, both in black gowns with hoods in the colors of the university. The flags of the dozens of countries from which the graduating students came, countries on six continents, decorated the walls of the hall - the university was proud of its long tradition of fostering international understanding. The American flag was in the center at the back of the platform, flanked by the State flag and the University insignia, and the flags of the nations which were home to the recipients of the honorary degrees being granted that day. The motto of the university was inscribed on the wall above the flags: Strength in Diversity; Harmony in Action.

"This is the last year of the twenty-first century's seventh decade," the Dean read from his notes. "During these seventy years, and especially in the years since the Thousand Awakenings, many individuals, groups and organizations have undertaken numerous initiatives to bring peace to our troubled world. Few initiatives have succeeded like those of the two degree recipients we now honor." Jackie and Nick, sitting together on the platform in the front row, engaged the audience in a radiance of heart energy.

"I ask Jacqueline Louise Cameron and Nicholas Lawrence Cameron to come forward please." Jackie and Nick stood and walked together, hand in hand, to their position beside the Dean, at the center of the platform facing the audience. Their black academic gowns made the thirty-five centimeter difference in their heights even more striking.

"I will speak of the two together, and we bestow their degrees together, not because they are husband and wife, but because they have worked together to enliven a world-wide energy of peace. Some consider their contributions to be in different realms of science: Health Science and Omniontolgy, the new science of being. They do not make that distinction, however, and have merged what seem like different disciplines into one. They take as the common platform of their work, the scientifically demonstrated fact that humanity is a single entity within a greater life.

"The Camerons tell me they were on retreat in the Canadian Rockies some twenty years ago when they conceived the idea of the Global Network For Light. Many in our audience, I know, are personally familiar with the Network, as are millions of people in all twenty-five regions of the world. If it is not familiar to you, think of a fiber-optic network that surrounds the planet carrying the light of the Love Impulse. Each time a node is added to the network –

that is, when another person enrolls in the Global Network For Light with the intention to radiate the Light of Love through a group service meditation – the light is amplified throughout the world. Of course, we do not need fiber-optics. As the Camerons and other scientists have shown us, The Network For Light produces an animation of the energy field of the entity we call humanity."

There was no need for the Dean to explain further how the Network functioned. The principles of the human energy field and the Love Impulse were common knowledge among high school graduates in most of the world. The Dean continued with the citation. "The Camerons say it took them about three months, following their retreat, to construct a strong and clear pattern of thought that would guide the manifestation of the Network concept. After that, they say, 'it just happened.' Well, what 'just happened' over the past twenty years was a global group of some five million dedicated participants clustered around forty centers – called Inspiration Centers – actively living the purpose of the Network.

"How does all this just happen? Their co-workers tell us, when the Camerons speak about the Network, people are attracted magnetically to contribute their radiance. People and resources seem to coagulate naturally around the message of peace and the quality of love the Camerons live. Their message gains strength from the scientific evidence that underpins their work.

"Although the Camerons, and now many others, inspire the work, the Network grows organically without a hierarchical structure. The network's purpose is the animating authority; its participants meet its administrative needs voluntarily. Whenever there are questions about how best to proceed, whether at the level of the individual, a local group, or the whole, participants always refer to the intuitive plane of pure reason for guidance.

"The Camerons brought an impressive set of credentials to their leadership of the Network." The Dean turned toward Jackie as he described her university studies in esoteric psychology, her initial counseling work after university, her human energy research and healing work with Alain, and then her traveling teaching clinics. "When she and her husband conceived the Global Network For Light, Jacqueline Cameron's clinical work was an integral part of the action. In each of the forty Inspiration Centers, Ms. Cameron established a model Clinic For Health and Healing. These model clinics have up to thirty satellite clinics each, where her energy-based health and healing modules are practiced, taught and refined. The clinics serve the purpose of the Network by enhancing the ability of their clients to contribute ever more purely to the Light of Love.

"It is widely acknowledged that the clinics represent the leading edge of the health and healing arts and sciences. They are centers of high competence and brilliant innovation, as well as centers of operational excellence." The Dean continued with details of the pivotal leadership role Jackie had played in developing, with her co-workers, the clinical modalities, the performance standards, and the operating processes which made the clinics so successful.

"Many national and international organizations have recognized her work for the betterment of the human condition. They have also recognized the special qualities she brings to every person she touches. Let me read to you what the British Minister of Human Resources wrote about Jacqueline Cameron. 'She has the courage of a lion and the gentleness of a lamb. She has the persistence of a redwood tree, yet is as sensitive as a willow leaf to the breezes of change. And in all of that, her devotion to her patients, her students, and her co-workers is unshakable. She is truly an angel of peace.'

"Mr. President, I commend to you, for the degree of Doctor of Science, Honoris Causa, Jacqueline Louise Cameron." The President presented the parchment to Jackie and shook her hand as the Dean placed the hood over her shoulders, to the applause of the audience and her husband.

The Dean then turned to Nick and spoke briefly about his early education in philosophy, then described his work as a journalist and leading peace activist. "He focused on bringing together people of different faiths in the context of the emerging new religion. Mr. Cameron has written that the new religion has no hierarchy of authority," the Dean read, "no dogma, no boundaries of exclusion. It is a religion that asks people to learn together and to seek within themselves the underlying truths of life. In the new religion, there are diverse approaches to learning, yet harmony among them. There is, above all, a seeking of peace through living the oneness of soul."

"In 2045," the dean continued, "Mr. Cameron began making a documentary based on his research in countries which, after centuries of conflict, were still not peaceful. He dug into the root causes of conflict and sought paths to conflict resolution, from the perspective of the unifying fact of the human energy field. In 2050, he completed his now famous work, *Our One Life*, a remarkable tour de force that is still turning heads and hearts, and indeed, triggering actions, toward the peace of unity. It has become a touchstone for all workers for peace.

"Mr. Cameron's role in the creation of the Global Network For Light was a natural outgrowth of his work for peace. His intellectual leadership was instrumental in formulating how the Network would operate and in setting out its initial strategies. His international reputation as a writer and peace activist brought large crowds to the initial organizing conferences; his inspiring speeches expressed clearly and powerfully the directional soul impressions his mind registered and translated. According to his co-workers at the Network, his presence inspires in them a zest for living their highest life purpose and enlivens in them a deep love for humanity. His optimism and his joyful energy is contagious, they say, making their workplace a paradise.

"The Network has taken most of Mr. Cameron's energies since he and his wife founded it, but he has continued to write and broadcast to extend the reach and strengthen the implementation of his central theme of spiritual unity and peace. Several organizations have given him their awards for his outstanding leadership in the cause of world peace. Now we recognize him as an inspiring visionary and a man of action, an intuitive scientist and a man of the humanities, a citizen of the world and a man of the people.

"Mr. President, I commend to you, for the degree of Doctor of Science, Honoris Causa, Nicholas Lawrence Cameron." To sustained applause, the Dean hooded Nicholas as the President presented the parchment to him, shook his hand and thanked him for his work.

Nick then leaned down to wrap his arms around Jackie. She rose up on her toes and they kissed, to the delight of the audience.

When they sat down, she whispered, "Nicholas, I am so grateful to all those people who created this moment. The groups in every country, all our friends, our parents, Grandpa Mac. And I couldn't have built the first clinic without the inheritance from Mama and Dollard. The clinics are their legacy, Nick, their spirit brought to life."

The President then stepped again to the lectern and introduced Nicholas as the Commencement speaker for the day. Without written notes, Nicholas slipped easily into a conversational mode and connected immediately with the audience. He spoke about the progress of peace in the world and the promise of a brighter future for humanity, emphasizing the inherent nature of peace in the kingdom of souls.

When he finished and the applause had subsided, the President stepped forward to conclude the afternoon's proceedings. "As most of you know, our Faculty of Human Energy Sciences includes one of the Regional Centers of the Global Network For Light. I invite the Drs. Cameron to close our Commencement exercise by leading us in contributing our energy of love to the Global Network."

Nearly everyone in the audience was familiar with the procedure since the Global Network Service Meditation had become a standard practice in almost every auditorium in the region. They all put their attention on the Network insignia placed on the arch above the platform. They tuned their mental focus to a thought of joining hearts in a global livance, imbuing humanity with love. The heart energy of the audience blended and harmonized with the love vibration held by hundreds of groups which the Global Network had linked around the world. The vibration amplified with each additional participant and radiated its love quality through and through the human family. For those who chose to respond to the radiation, it was an opportunity to rise to a greater awareness of the oneness of humanity. That increased awareness, brought into daily action, was the path to peace.

After the commencement ceremonies, there was a reception in the garden of the Chair of the Board of Trustees. Jackie and Nick and the other two honorees, the Chair and his wife, and the President all formed a receiving line, greeting and chatting with faculty and some thirty or forty invited guests. The guests included Gwynneth and her husband, Arthur, who had come from Dartmouth where they were both senior professors. "Our big brother is now a doctor, is he? Well, you both deserve it. Congratulations." Gwynneth and Arthur gave them both big hugs.

"What a life you've had, the two of you," said Arthur. "What is it that drives you? How have you overcome all the obstacles you have encountered?"

"It's simple, in a way, Arthur," Nick said, throwing an arm over his brother-in-law's shoulder. "Just accept that soul is in charge; personality responds."

"Personality is the agent of soul," Jackie added. "Soul is the principle, the master within. Who we really are. Hear the vibration of soul and align with it. Then you can face life's turmoil with ease."

"Hear the vibration of soul? Easier said than done, I guess."

"It takes attention and practice, Arthur, but it's the only way to go."

"And soul has jurisdiction over personality, you say. Okay, what is my soul doing here in my personality anyway?" Many people were asking such questions, especially since a plethora of books about soul appeared during the first half of the century.

"As souls, we are incarnating here in form, torn between our attraction to this form, our status as humans, if you like, and our desire to be released from that attraction and return to oversoul," Jackie said.

"So, how come we are attracted to form?"

"That connection was engendered many aeons ago, Arthur, because we - our line of entities – decided we should experiment with form as a way of aligning more easily with our ultimate destiny. We decided to try to govern ourselves independently of the 'Great Chorus'."

"Whoa! That gets a little above my pay grade," Arthur laughed.

"But, Arthur, it plays out right here in our everyday lives." Jackie always tried to bring the abstract reality down to objective reasoning.

"How do you mean?"

"Have you ever wondered why we humans get embroiled in emotional turmoil?"

"It's just human nature, isn't it?"

"Evolving human nature, maybe. You know how we seem to learn most from what seem to be our worst experiences."

"True enough."

"Now, think of that turmoil as purely related to our form life. Learning to handle turmoil is learning to be master of our own lives. And that is a reflection of soul learning to release its attachment to form."

"So I'm just soul's puppet, I suppose." Arthur laughed at the idea. "Well, thank you very much, soul.

"Your souls are obviously getting free," Gwynneth said, giving Jackie and Nick a hug and a kiss. "We are very proud of you. Grandpa Mac would be especially proud."

"Thanks, Gwyn." Nick gave his sister an extra hug.

"We have to go along now. Arthur has to meet with a colleague here at the university."

"And Gwyn is going to use the library. We'll see you later at the restaurant. Don't forget, you are our guests tonight."

After Gwynneth and Arthur left, Jackie and Nick found a secluded corner of the garden and came together in a long and heart-stirring embrace. "I wish our families could have been here, Nick. Mama especially, and Nana and Papa Rivera."

"Yes, and Monique would say, 'So, what's next?'"

"She would. And your parents, Nick. We'll visit them in their care home as soon as we get back. They'll want to see these fancy parchments."

As they eased apart with a kiss, they heard a faintly familiar voice behind them. "Congratulations to both of you."

They turned. "Korry?" Nick whispered. The man was dressed in a light blue suit.

"Korry – it really is you." Jackie exclaimed. "What are you doing here?"

"I'm with the catering service," he smiled.

"Trail maintenance. Catering service. Sure." Nick laughed.

"I've come to offer you our congratulations."

"You say 'our'? Is that the royal 'our'?"

"Your group," Korry replied. "We see you are on track - both of you. We are ready to continue our support for your next endeavors."

Chapter Twenty-Eight

The Final Years: Continuing Action

"Think of the choices we've made, Doreen, trying to find that preferred way that aligns with soul's purpose." Jackie and Doreen were reminiscing over a photo album.

"Too bad our choices aren't laid out for us from the start and we could just follow the arrows. I wish I could have known my life's path when I was born instead of stumbling along all these ninety years."

Jackie laughed. "But then imagine knowing where you are going as soon as you are born. What fun would that be?"

"We have had some fun, haven't we Jackie? Especially you and Nick." She paused, eyes softening. "Lloyd and I – it was fun, but in a simpler way. We were very happy with our lives together."

"You do miss him, don't you Doreen?"

"I do. I miss his curiosity. I miss his attention to detail. I miss talking to him at breakfast. And before we go to sleep. And the touch of his fingers on my cheek. Yes, I do miss him, Jackie." She was silent for a moment, deep in thought. Then, "It won't be long now. I'll probably be around here a few more years, and then I'll see him again."

"So, what did you and Doreen do today?" Nick and Jackie were sitting side by side on their patio, watching the changing colors of the clouds above the setting sun.

"We went for a walk around the Common, and then just sat in her garden and had tea." Jackie leaned over toward Nick, took his upper arm in both her hands, and kissed him on the cheek. "We talked about destiny."

"Ninety years olds talking about destiny - that must have been interesting."

"Don't laugh. We've got it all figured out."

"Oh, have you? And what, my love, will be our destiny? Eternal youth?"

"No such luck, dear soul. It's eternal searching."

"Like, 'Where did I leave my reading glasses'?"

She ran a knuckle over his ribs. "Be serious. We were talking about how soul matures as we accept its will in our lives – how we bring its refined vibration into human actions. How we come to express soul's purpose. That kind of destiny."

"So, destiny as determined by soul."

"More or less."

Nick wasn't quite ready to be serious. "Like, soul said, 'Open teaching clinics around the world.' So, you did as part of the Network. Then, when we were old enough to retire, soul said, 'Not yet, Jackie. You and Nick work together for another twenty-five years and start a new kind of university. Is that it?"

"You know better than that."

"Yes, I know how it goes. If we can tune to soul's abstract impulse toward the idea of oneness and register it in our intuition as an ideal, our mental field might pick it up and translate it into thoughts that we condense into concrete action. Soul's ultimate destiny is a given. How we personalities align with that inevitable stream shapes the pattern of a particular personality life."

"Doreen and I discussed something else that happens on the way to our destiny. Think about souls becoming closely entwined like ours are."

"We become one within our hearts."

"And something else."

204

"What?"

"Do you remember, in the Rockies, how we came to the idea of the Global Network? I know it was forty-five years ago, my dear, and with your memory slipping . . ."

"My memory is not slipping. I remember exactly. I was wondering how to link up with all the people in the world who work for peace."

"And so was I – exactly the same thing. Now, here is another test. Do you remember what happened after we received our honorary doctorates?"

"We met Korry."

"The next day."

"We spent the day at the Unus Retreat Center. Our friends from the Faculty of Human Energy Sciences took us to their round meditation building."

"And?"

"And we meditated of course.

"And?"

"Okay, I see what you're getting at. We both had the same idea – at the same moment. Just like in the Rockies. It was immediate, wasn't it. I remember you turning to look at me just as I turned to look at you."

"A oneness of two minds."

"Right. Our integrated minds penetrated the same sphere of intelligence which had precipitated our earlier ideas about energies and health, but this time with greater depth and breadth."

"Exactly. Two brains, but one integrated mind, one shared thought. Destinies entwined."

"But not identical, Jackie."

"No. But the shape of both are altered and tending toward identical."

"Interesting how it works. The mind becomes so steady in the light . . ."

"Our alignment with soul so complete . . ."

"That we were able to probe more deeply than ever before into the highest frequencies of the mental plane." As he spoke, Nick registered that higher mental frequency and continued, "Our melded intuition drew out of the vast Universal Intelligence, just that substance which our minds could resonate to and comprehend."

"Of course it was a highly abstract impulse. The plan of action came later."

"We also registered an imperative which was embedded in the idea – the action had to follow. We simply had to make it happen. And we did, Jackie. We did."

"So those are the two things Doreen and I were discussing. We approach our ultimate destiny only as we align with soul's will. And entwined souls tend act in concert."

"And that's us."

"That's us." As the conversation stirred their memories, their hands slipped together with interlacing fingers and they sat in silence, their minds tracing the events first set in motion in the Rockies with the idea of the Global Network For Light, followed by the idea arising during Unus Retreat Center meditation.

The Global Network was based on the reality of the correspondence between the energy system of an individual human being and the energy system of humanity. The entity - humanity - is a system of energy fields, just as a human being is a system of energy fields; the two systems are analogous and they interact – the whole affects the part, and vice versa. That means, of course, there is just one all-encompassing field. Hence, the combination of Health Sciences and Omniontology - Jackie's human energy health and healing for individuals, and Nick's leadership of the Global Group Service Meditation for the soul of humanity.

The One Field idea was not new. Mystics had been speaking about oneness for a few thousand years; theoretical scientists had been formulating the concept for a few hundred years. By the end of the twentieth century, scientists and energy practitioners were gathering evidence of the interactions among the parts - implying the whole. During the twenty-first century, acceptance of the One Field idea had become widespread and was the basis for many streams of thought and action.

The particular stream of thought Jackie and Nick had registered led them to manifest concretely the key principle: to heal the whole is to heal the part - and vice versa. Whether at the level of the part or the whole, 'to heal' means to clarify and refine the flows of energy, to reduce the static and distortions, and to tune to ever higher vibrations. It was a stream of thought which registered with them, not as a theory, but as a matter of fundamental intelligence, a fact, a concrete reality which entered into the whole of their beings and permeated their every action.

It registered in Jackie and Nick, in particular, because it resonated with the patterns of knowing they had accumulated in their earlier experiences - Jackie's development of health and healing modules, Nick's philosophical journalism. Their combined intelligence, animated by their alignment with the Great Center of Knowing, precipitated such strong thought forms that, when they materialized them in broadcast productions, in group service meditations, and in clinical procedures, their thoughts infiltrated easily into the minds of millions worldwide. Groups were drawn quickly and easily to their message, and thoughts became actions. The seeds of knowing - that is, the potential for understanding - had over the aeons been widely scattered, awaiting the light needed for germination. The light of the couple's work produced many sprouting seeds.

Now, as they approached their ninetieth birthdays, Nick and Jackie could see their original work being enriched and extended by groups everywhere. The multi-lingual, holographic technology of space station communications centers, and the techniques and programs developed by the Global Network For Light, combined to make a powerful force which was moving the world.

The Unus Retreat Center meditation expanded the sensitivity of their mental fields still further and they penetrated the Universal Intelligence to a level well beyond the reach they had previously perceived. Within five years, they had translated their deeper insight into a new kind of university, the Fifth Kingdom Academy. Its mission was to train soul-sensitive groups of adults to see and modulate energy flows and patterns in the individual, the group, and the community, in order to bring greater energy sensitivity to those leading the work for peace and harmony in the world. "Our purpose," Nick had said to the Academy's first student group, "is to accelerate our arrival at soul's ultimate destiny. Our theme is: 'Thy will be done, on earth as it is in heaven.' Our organizing energy is love."

The training demanded strong and refined personalities that could handle the high frequency energies the groups engaged. "The density of the personality is the limiting factor," Nick told the students. "So, in this program, there are only disciples with a long-time habit of training to refine the physical, emotional and mental bodies."

Ten years after the Unus retreat, there were branches of the Academy attached to the Global Network For Light in fourteen regions. Twenty years later, as the new century dawned, there were over a thousand students enrolled in the full-time three year, basic course of study, thirty in the full-time advanced course in London, and another five thousand studying part time. Some six thousand graduates of the three-year basic program were at work around the world. Jackie held the energy for the internal matters of the Academy; Nick, the external. Both engaged the advanced students in their studies. The teaching and administrative work was organized as a non-hierarchical cooperative, in the same manner as the Network.

"It has been a long road, Nicholas dear. Can we actually retire now?"

"What about the eternal searching? Is it over?"

"Eternal. I guess that's the operative word."

"I suppose then we'll never retire from the search, just from our worldly duties."

"Surely at ninety, Nick, our worldly duties are over."

"Just one more duty, my love. Remember our date in Japan in August."

"It is our pleasure to have with us today our colleagues, Jacqueline and Nicholas Cameron." The tiny Japanese woman was a graduate of the Academy. She spoke impeccable English, the product of many years of international travel on behalf of the International Peace Foundation of Japan. "Through their inspiring idealism and the very practical programs and technologies of the Global Network for Light and the Fifth Kingdom Academy, millions of us around the world have begun to know and, in the deepest way, to live the fact that we are, in our essence, complex fields of divine energy. We are not human animals, as many scientists once had us believing, but human souls in the arms of one Great Being. In our essence . . ." The speaker paused a moment and became a brilliant light which infused the gathering. "We are Peace; we are Love; we are One." She was addressing an audience of hundreds, including senior diplomats from every United Nations country, at the annual observances at the Hiroshima memorial shrine.

"The Camerons, working together and through their Fifth Kingdom Foundation, have helped us to know that the impulse toward the peace of Oneness is soul's imperative, and the peace of soul is the natural condition of humankind. They have helped us, millions of us throughout the world, learn how to live that condition for the benefit of humankind.

"In this year of 2095, the one hundred and fiftieth anniversary of the bomb that shook the world's conscience, we present to Jacqueline and Nicholas Cameron the Hiroshima Award for the Advancement of Humanity."

In the Light Room of the London office of the Network and the Academy, Nick and Jackie stood before the plenum on which they had carefully placed the Hiroshima award. The award was a sculpture featuring a quartz crystal placed at the point of an upsweeping glass arrow. The crystal refracted rainbows onto the faces of the office's fifty workers who were arrayed around the plenum. By holographic means, three thousand workers and students around the world participated in the meeting, some of them in a timed delayed re-creation.

The pair stood beside the plenum, both still able, in spite of their years, to hold themselves straight and relaxed, a reflection of their own message of inner and outer health. Their combined fields of light immediately gathered the group energetically. Jackie spoke first. "Dear friends – dear colleagues – you all know, I am sure, this award recognizes the work of all of us, in the Global Network For Light and the Fifth Kingdom Academy and beyond, who are dedicated in service of soul's healing impulse."

Nick took her hand and continued, "The award speaks to our future intent as much as it recognizes our past. Look at its design – the arrow pointing always upward toward the One that we are, toward the freedom of the planet, toward the essence of Life. Toward our destiny."

"And now, dear friends, the time has come for us to speak of our future intent." Jackie's smile embraced all three thousand. She linked her arm through Nick's. "Nick and I have decided it is time to step down from the work which has been our preoccupation for the last twenty-five years and leave it to you younger folk to carry the movement forward into the next century. Note, I said we will 'step down', not 'leave.' "

"Step down means," Nick continued, "we will not engage directly in the activities of the Academy and the Network. We will, however, continue to hold our highest purpose and our unity in our hearts - always. Do not ever forget we are a group with deep ties and a continuity beyond this incarnation."

"Tomorrow," Jackie told them, "as a way of beginning the withdrawal, Nick and I will leave on a vacation, our retirement present to ourselves. Our destination is the same Italian alpine village where we spent our honeymoon." The assembly applauded. They included a few friends the couple had known since their twenties, as well as some their friends' children and grandchildren.

"Yes, and Jackie thinks we are going to climb to the same ridges and lookouts we did sixty-five years ago. Please, folks, pray for me." Nick looked at Jackie and laughed.

"We have an hour here in Aosta, Nick, before we catch our ride to the village. Let's stop at the tourism office across the street. I'd like to pick up a topographical map."

"You really think we are going climbing, don't you?"

"Just in case. How's your Italian? Shall I speak to them?"

"Good morning, Madame et Monsieur," the young man behind the desk greeted them.

Clever, Nick thought. The man anticipated their two national origins. "Good morning," said Nick. Then, looking at the young man more carefully, he frowned, puzzled. "Korry?"

Jackie gasped. It was indeed Korry.

"It's impossible," Nick exclaimed "Are you ageless?"

"What does age mean, my friends?" Korry raised one eyebrow. "Your search is eternal, didn't you say?"

"But Korry, what are you doing here?"

"Why, I'm helping people with their journeys of course."

"A travel agent?"

"You might say so. I have a suggestion for you, my colleagues."

"For our journey?" Jackie enquired.

"Yes. For the final few steps."

"Our final years?"

"Yes." Korry engaged the total of their beings with the energy of love. Then: "Be awake." The words were like a flash of electrical fire that coursed through them from head to toe.

They were sitting at the first lookout on the same trail they had hiked on their honeymoon. The trail was wider than when they last visited, there were more hikers, and the valley below had many more buildings in places where yesterday there had been pastures. The mountain atmosphere, they noticed - the space of quiet - was much the same as before. They also noticed the soaring of their spirit was much higher than before. Their energy sensitivity had matured and become more discriminating.

"We have more to do, Jackie." The space of quiet was not a passive space.

"I know, Nick. We are not finished yet." Both of them knew they were involved in an esoteric action and they still had responsibilities. "Korry's words, Nick. Our mission is . . . How to say . . ."

"Yes, Love, it is hard to comprehend. It is a still larger action than we had imagined. Moreover, we have a purpose-focused esoteric group behind us now. We can touch a wider reach of Intelligence and do much more."

"There are assignments waiting for us, my dear old man. I guess we've been too busy getting things done to notice there is more to do."

"Well, my dear Jacqueline, now that we are retired, we can stop all that old work. It is time to focus our alignment with our new group's purpose, and direct our radiance of love and will toward the call of humanity's soul."

"It's our ninety-fifth birthday, Love. Did you remember?"

"Yes, my dear old man, and I think it may be our last."

"Are you ready to return?"

"Quite ready, Nick. Ninety-five years is enough for me."

"I guess we'll have to leave this new century to its fate."

"Others are at work, mon amour. The world will be just fine."

"We will come back soon enough – to check."

"Soon enough."

"We are blessed, are we not, Jackie? We have had a long and healthy life."

"And the privilege of being able to serve. Do you think we served well, mon amour?"

"Yes, Love. Quite well."

"Then, my dear Nicholas, we can go home."

FREEING THE LIGHT OF SOUL

Chapter Twenty-Nine

The Release

"Aiya, it is almost time for your release. Are you ready?" Ohruu's gathering up had already been completed, Jacqueline having passed away several months earlier. Aiya was still connected to Nicholas and was tending to the last few threads of life which were still attached to the Nicholas etheric body.

"I won't be long, Ohruu. Our reunion is near."

On his last day, Nick rested comfortably in his reclining chair in the sunroom of their home. He knew he had only hours before he would gain release from his earthly form. He had suffered no illness and no pain in his final days – merely a gradual decrease in vitality and a noticeably weakening heartbeat. The couple's long-time housekeeper looked in on him at regular intervals, respecting his wish for solitude.

In the morning, he had spoken briefly with leaders of the Global Network For Light and the Fifth Kingdom Academy. He asked them to remove all signs of his and Jackie's involvement in the organization – no memorial tablets, no named buildings, nothing that would attach a personality to the work. "Let the purpose be the inspiration," he urged. "And honor the future, not the past. Jackie and I – as personalities - we are nothing. The group and its purpose are everything."

Now it was late morning and he asked his housekeeper to put his chair in the semi-recline position. She did so and left him to his final thoughts. There were still remnants of his urge to continue the work for peace. In the quiet, he consciously reconciled that urge with another – a different urge, a strengthening one, an urge fueled by Aiya's will to break free of form. The Love Impulse had driven his work for all of his adult life. It had infused his purpose, shaped his values, and energized him physically. He and Jackie, together as one, had learned to be an unusually clear personification of the Love Impulse. Now he was having some difficulty stepping out of its earthbound mission - there was so much still to do here and he still had strong attachments to the work.

The oversoul's call to return home grew louder, however, and it was an imperative to which Aiya responded by another break of the consciousness thread, making the soul's attraction to form almost non-existent. Aiya's incarnating purpose had been achieved; the form life no longer pulled attention away from soul's natural home. The urge to return home was now the controlling polarity. It was that time of the cycle – a time to absorb and incorporate the outposts of soul's sentiency which were resident in the Nicholas persona. It was the prelude to soul's transition and reorientation to freedom. It was the time for soul's release from the constriction of form.

Aiya marshaled extra strength to effect the withdrawal. In a few hours it would be time to break another filament of its life-giving aspect from the physical body. Then the body would start to come to rest, its rhythmic signals slowing and fading, its vibrance diminishing. The pranic energy of the dense physical body would then begin to drain away. As the vitality of the physical body diminished, the restitution of the etheric substance - the vital body - would begin. Aiya had gathered the substance from the planetary etheric body to hold the Nicholas physical body atoms in form, and it would now become reabsorbed to its origin. The dense physical body, having served its purpose and now no longer vital, would begin its restitution to its earthly elements.

As Aiya went about the completion of this incarnate journey, Nicholas began correspondingly to relax his mental engagement with the affairs of the peacemaking organizations which had engaged his attention for so many years. He breathed out the last vibrations of tension and breathed in the peace of his withdrawing soul. He felt the strength draining from his muscles. He was ready, in fact almost impatient, to move on – ready for his consciousness to leave his physical body.

He turned his head toward the bay window, which looked out on his favorite corner of the garden where the roses were blooming. Jackie had brought her healing touch to the garden and the roses had responded gratefully. Their color and fragrance permeated the air, both in the garden and in the house where bouquets filled vases in every room. He immersed himself in their beauty. This will be difficult to leave behind, he thought momentarily, knowing of course he would perceive even greater beauty when he became free of the distorting filter of physical form.

He looked forward to that form-free condition, knowing its potential from the many times he had achieved a continuity of consciousness. Still, he found himself questioning whether in fact he had fulfilled his life's work. Nicholas was aware the habit of his personal will was strong, even at the end. How strange was this mix of uncertainty about completion and anticipation of what was next.

Anticipation took over. All the brightness of his heart's deepest desire pervaded his consciousness - soul's urge to be free of the noise of the human experience gained the foreground. Aiya was ready to move and Nicholas knew it. In a last rush of energy, his mind constructed a summary of his life, presented in brief flashes of the people and events that represented essential meanings:

~ His family heritage – the strong, healthy physical body of the Cameron genes, the emotional stability from the nurturing of a loving family, the example of a long family tradition of public service and accomplishment, the opportunity of a good formal education, and the gift of early independence.

~ His dear Jacqueline - her words of love at the sidewalk café in Paris, their absolute dedication and final merging into a bright single light in the Rocky Mountains.

~ His mentors – his parents, Grandpa Mac, the ship's engineer, Alain L'Heureux. And Korry.

~ His Unus meditation with Jacqueline - their unified urge to action as fully ensouled personalities.

Nicholas let his mind elaborate the meeting with Korry on the trail in the Rocky Mountains. He and Jacqueline knew at the time that something deep within each of them had been altered, something that had tuned them to a higher octave of life. They spoke of it as feeling they had been rewired or reshaped in order to play their purpose note more precisely and more strongly. They later understood the quality of their work as journalist and healer had made their light esoterically noticeable, and Korry had come to enroll them in a greater purpose, a larger enterprise – the enterprise of the group of souls Korry attracted – the ashram. In their mountain meeting, he had wrapped them, clothed them, infused them with the ashram's light. Then he sent them on their way to act with the heightened vibrance they now shared with their inner group of brothers and sisters.

The sequence of images in Nicholas' mind became a holographic picture of his soul's achievement – a radiant appearance in human form – manifesting, in concert with Jacqueline and their inner group, the light of love in the dark corners of the world.

There was a gentle knock on the door. "Please come," he managed to respond. The housekeeper and some members of Lloyd and Doreen's family came into the room – their son and daughter and their spouses, three of their grandchildren and their spouses, and two of their great grandchildren. Lloyd and Doreen had treated Nicholas and Jacqueline as members of their family. Their children and grandchildren knew them as Uncle Nick and Auntie Jackie.

All were smiling as they entered. Each carried a rose which they placed in Nick's arms - just as they had done with Jacqueline, Nicholas remembered.

"We are so happy for you today, Uncle Nick," said the ten-year-old brightly. "We will miss you, but we know you are going home."

"Yes, you are going to be with Auntie Jackie," chimed the eight year old behind a big grin. "And please say 'hello' to her for us, won't you?"

"And that we love her," added the ten year old. "Of course she knows that, doesn't she."

"Yes, Annie, she does know it, but I'll tell her anyway," Nicholas responded in a forced whisper. His voice grew weaker even as he spoke. Looking into the eyes of each of them in turn, he smiled and said, "Thank you for coming. All of you. And for coming at this moment."

"We knew it was time, Uncle Nick," the daughter said. "We have been waiting in the garden chapel until we knew to come. Now we are here to share in the celebration of your release."

"Please make yourselves comfortable," Nick whispered. "Everyone relax, please, and celebrate the passing with joy."

"Is it time to start the music, Uncle Nick? Chopin?"

"Not just yet, Andrew." Nick's voice was barely audible and he struggled to ease his position in the chair. Andrew's wife helped him get comfortable, propping pillows around him. "First, I want to tell all of you how much you have meant to me over the years, and to Jacqueline." His words emerged from his lips one at a time. "You have made us part of your family by your love and your care, and by your work to bring your soul vibrations into harmony with ours. You have become our family, in esoteric fact as well as in outward appearance. And you know, don't you, we will continue to be family - forever."

"Yes, we know, Uncle Nick. Forever."

"Good." He breathed in the perfume of the roses, then whispered, "And now the Chopin, Andrew." He closed his eyes and smiled, letting the music play through his being like a breeze playing the strings of a harp. It relaxed his persona grip, making it easier for soul to overcome the last vestige of human consciousness.

With a surge of will, Aiya withdrew soul's consciousness aspect from the center in the head, and then finalized the withdrawal from the physical body by abstracting the remainder of the life aspect from the heart.

Freed from the prison of the physical body, Aiya held consciousness on the plane of the mental sheath. From that plane, the soul turned its attention toward the few shadows of human desire which remained on the edges of its mental awareness. This focus of attention brought forth an intensification of the light of oversoul, which dissipated the shadows, leaving the mental body in its full fineness of clarity. The light was brilliant and all-encompassing.

With the mental body now absolutely clear, Aiya heard the strike of a chord, a sound of fire emanating from the oversoul, which broke open and discarded the sheath of the mental body, leaving Aiya free of any veiling substance, free to stand in the center of core consciousness. Free to stand in soul's true identity.

Aiya was not immediately aware of this freedom, not fully in touch with the shift of condition, not fully aware of the reality. It was necessary to shake off the dead leaves of the perception acquired during the physical form experience. It was like waking from a deep sleep in a strange bedroom – puzzled, needing to take stock, needing to remember who and where you were.

As Aiya began to see the reality of soul identity, the unhampered vibration of Presence resonated in Aiya's core being and broke through the curtain of uncertainty. It steadily erased the last sketches of illusion. The retrieval was complete. In the bright light of oversoul, Aiya knew a fresh clear quality of vibration. It was a case of stepping into a new home – yet one that was totally familiar.

Aiya recalled the stages of the long journey which led to the opening of the door of this new home:

~ The slow work - of the early hundreds of incarnations.

~ The more rapid progress during the several incarnations of the first millennium of the current era.

~ The quick pace of the six incarnations during the second millennium.

~ The just concluded final human expedition at the beginning of the third millennium.

~ The extension of the merger with Ohruu at the wedding.

~ The testing and tempering of soul expression during the journalist years.

~ The alignment with the purpose of the ashram.

Following the release from the Nicholas form, in the new freedom from illusion, the vibrance of the group sounded aloud in Aiya's core. In the harmonics, Aiya recognized the presence of those who were close in past incarnations - an esoteric family. Nicholas had become aware of the fact of his membership in an esoteric group a short time after the meeting with Korry in the Rockies, and Korry had mentioned it explicitly to Nicholas and Jacqueline just after the Commencement ceremony. Aiya's recognition, however, was immediate and completely lucid. Here was a group of old friends that related like Nicholas' group of friends and co-workers on earth related, only more closely.

The group sounded the clear note of a joyous homecoming, absorbing the Aiya core in the resonance of the attractive force of their love, a process of assimilating, unifying and strengthening. And now the harmonics included Aiya's note as it joined the chorus.

Aiya stood fully in the consciousness of Being. In its core mental atom, the soul recognized it could communicate directly in thought patterns with the group. It had merely to formulate a thought – like speaking to oneself – and it registered as a mind vibration in others who were on the same wavelength. Similarly, Aiya registered the thought vibrations of others by attending to them and adjusting soul's tuning mechanism.

Ohruu's particular vibration was the first that came into Aiya's sphere and the tuning was easy. "It has been a ride, Aiya." Ohruu radiated their common frequency and their thoughts were instantaneously integrated.

"And what a ride, Ohruu. An interdimensional escape."

The other members of the community registered a common frequency, gathering and chatting as though at a family picnic: the immortal cores of Lloyd, Doreen, the ship's engineer, Monique, Alain, and others who had been very close in several earlier incarnations. And Korry was there. Korry - the mentor. Korry – the immortal core of Grandpa Mac.

A central note anchored the collective vibrations of the gathering, a note that swung Aiya even more strongly into the center of the stream of action of the group's purpose. It was to hold him forever in a place of resonance with the group. And, equally, it held Ohruu, the two as a single light, a node in the network of the group's connecting energies.

The group's purpose manifested as a thought form, which Aiya and Ohruu registered with increasing clarity. They saw, in the context of their group's purpose, that much of the world had moved into a considerable resonance with the Love Impulse since the Thousand Awakenings in 2005. There was a strengthening global alignment with the attractive force of the Impulse, with its urge to unity, with its call to know and express the fact of the oneness of humanity, the oneness of all life.

In some parts of the world, however, there still remained large pockets of separateness that showed up as violent tribal, religious, or ethnic skirmishes, as sexual exploitation, greed, and mindless assertion of power. For more than a century, the international community had poured resources and human effort into combating these evils – indeed, Jacqueline and Nicholas had been a part of these efforts. Yet resistance to oneness persisted. As the light of humanity brightened, however, the dark stains of separateness became more visible and the work of cleansing could become more focused. Now it was the mission of the group, in which Aiya and Ohruu served, to bring, through its esoteric action, an inpouring of love to replace the toxic diet which these unfortunate people consumed. The group's first goal was to break open the hard shell of fear for self, which enclosed their hearts and minds.

After the welcoming, Korry addressed the two. "By your persistence over the millennia, you have achieved the ultimate goal of the cycle of human incarnation. You have liberated yourselves from the attracting force of matter, and your light can now shine freely through the human form. In doing so, you have been serving Life's evolutionary purpose." Aiya and Ohruu understood.

"Now it is time for you to prepare for the next phase of your service." Korry embraced Aiya and Ohruu in a substantial light that conveyed the group purpose with brilliant clarity. Within that context, their minds registered the agenda they would follow in this, their natural environment. Except when called to a specific group action, deep meditation – orientating to their higher source - would be their continuing posture. They would dwell in the place of quiescent learning. Alignment with the higher frequencies of evolution would be their overriding priority.

The immediate aligning step would be to strengthen and consolidate the mastery of form they had achieved during the Nicholas and Jacqueline excursion. When that mastery had been solidified, they would be led to see their greater responsibilities. Korry would introduce them for the first time to the Inner Courtyard of the ashram where they would absorb a new relationship with the group and take a new position of service.

"That is when your work will begin in earnest," Korry said. "That is when you will be called to an even greater task than your present perception can even imagine."

The two absorbed his aura of action.

"In the meantime, prepare yourself. Our way is always forward."

The joy of soul's voice
sounds
in each moment
of
freedom.

ISBN 141200453-5

9 781412 004534